Y0-BRF-896

THE FAMILY SECRET

THE FAMILY SECRET

An Anthology

▲

Edited by Jay David

Foreword by Migs Woodside
President, Children of Alcoholics Foundation

William Morrow and Company, Inc.
New York

Permissions, constituting a continuation of the copyright page,
appear on page 265.

Library of Congress Cataloging-in-Publication Data

The family secret : an anthology /
edited with a introduction by Jay David ; foreword by Migs Woodside.
p. cm.
ISBN 0-688-12067-9
1. Adult children of alcoholics—United States—Biography.
I. David, Jay.
HV5132.F37 1994
362.29'24'092273—dc20 94-4960
CIP

Printed in the United States of America

First Edition

1 2 3 4 5 6 7 8 9 10

BOOK DESIGNED BY OKSANA KUSHNIR

FOREWORD

Don't trust. Don't talk. Don't feel. This is the credo of children of alcoholics.

One out of every eight Americans is the child of an alcoholic. Through no fault of their own, this group comprises a distinctly high-risk population. There is no denying it: Children of alcoholics tend to become alcoholics themselves:

- Sons of alcoholic fathers are four times more likely to become future alcoholics.
- Daughters of alcoholic mothers are three times more likely to become future alcoholics.
- Women alcoholics are twice as likely as men to have been reared by two alcoholic parents, and daughters of alcoholics are more likely to marry alcoholics, thus unintentionally perpetuating the cycle of this family tragedy.

Growing up in a family touched by alcoholism can leave scars that last a lifetime. Physical and emotional problems begin for some children even before they are born. Mothers who abuse alcohol during pregnancy may bear children who suffer from fetal alcohol syndrome (FAS) or fetal alcohol effects (FAE). These children can have a wide range of problems, from facial abnormalities to mental retardation.

Young children of alcoholics may also show signs of emotional detachment, dependency, aggression, and low self-esteem. In school, they are more likely than other youngsters to have learning problems, to be hyperactive or delinquent, and are three times more likely to be expelled or to drop out. They also have higher rates of inpatient hospital stays and require more visits to physicians. Some studies show that there is a strong correlation between parental alcohol abuse and child abuse, eating disorders, and suicide.

One might think children from alcoholic families have a host of problems that keep them from functioning or coping with life's stresses. While it is true that one out of four children of alcoholic families in America will become an alcoholic, *three out of four* go on to lead successful, productive lives. Many children of alcoholics are "resilient"—they possess the human capacity to beat the odds—to do well in the face of adversity.

In fact, the people in this book typify resiliency. Their personal accounts clearly show the suffering, fear, and confusion caused by parental alcoholism. A painfully familiar refrain—characterized by guilt, anxiety, frustration, and sadness—courses through their stories, as it does through the lives of most children from alcoholic families. But these accounts show, too, that children of alcoholics can move from helplessness to hopefulness; from powerlessness to powerfulness.

These writers have an especially important story to tell, because *The Family Secret* is not just about sadness and pain. It is also about strength and hope. It shows the crucial need for help, and the revelation that can be startling to many children of alcoholic families: that they are not alone, and that they deserve and are worthy of help.

Perhaps, most important of all, *The Family Secret* shows that children touched by family alcoholism can have a happier and brighter future after all.

Migs Woodside
President
Children of Alcoholics Foundation

ACKNOWLEDGMENTS

My thanks go to researchers Laura Bergheim,
Christine Magginis, and Beth Pratt-Dewey.

Also I extend thanks to my editor, Zach Schisgal, for his labors at keeping this project going. Grace Dwyer-Olsen from the Children of Alcoholics Foundation came through for me and provided the art to spruce up the text.

CONTENTS

INTRODUCTION

Too often, research statistics must serve as the only record of the lives of children of alcoholics. One in ten Americans has the disease alcoholism. An estimated twenty-eight million children have at least one alcoholic parent. Children of alcoholics are three and one-half times more likely than others to become alcoholics themselves. But behind the numbers are millions of stories. Stories that show children—sad, bewildered, ashamed, angry, afraid, resentful, and hopeful. *The Family Secret* brings some of these stories together for the first time.

The book is divided into four parts, representing some of the broader truths about alcoholism: Families hide the disease from others; children living with alcoholic parents are commonly abused; alcoholic parents die early; and children of alcoholics are prone to abuse alcohol and drugs themselves. These generalizations pile up along with statistics until we forget people provide the raw data, an important issue when dealing with the disease of alcoholism. Every story is different and deserves a compassionate hearing. Yet each is, in some way, representative of typical events unfolding in households with an alcoholic parent everywhere in the United States.

Unlike many children of alcoholics, the people in this book beat the odds. Although most of them have attained what we recognize as success, their words prove that they never forget—and sometimes never overcome—the traumas of their childhoods. Years after they've left their homes or their parents are dead, they're still sifting through the pieces of their shattered childhoods.

Many of the authors in this anthology are either the children of famous parents, or have achieved fame themselves. It is sad to realize that, until recently, stories of childhood in an alcoholic family would rarely have been published unless written by someone who had achieved celebrity or was related to someone famous. But in addition to being among the few sources of writing on this important subject, these recollections by famous personalities also emphasize the ability of the human spirit to triumph over adversity. Even when these adult children of alcoholism realized that they had indeed inherited their parents' disease, they were determined not to suffer the same ugly fate they had seen their parents play out. Not only did these people survive their childhoods—they went on to great achievements in life.

For some of the authors, the scars have been healed, and they can look back at their parents with compassion. For others, the memories are still clearly painful. But none of the authors look back without wondering how much better their childhoods would have been if they had not had an alcoholic parent.

THE FAMILY SECRET

On this side
I'm confused, be-
wildered, and scared.
I wish I could talk
to our good friends.
On this side I'm
sad for my father
+ I wish it never
happened.

PART ONE

KEEPING THE FAMILY SECRET

Children of alcoholics learn to hide the problem.

▲

A child quickly learns to keep the family secret. Perhaps children of alcoholics sense how different their homes are from those of their friends. Sometimes children will just take their cues from the family. They become experts at hiding the secret of parental drinking and making excuses for outrageous behavior at their homes. Some act out of shame, a feeling that keeps kids from seeking the help they need. Others act from a sense of control—if everything appears normal, perhaps the situation will become OK. The habit of secrecy and avoiding problems often carries over into adulthood, even when the alcoholism doesn't.

DOREEN ROAM

from *The New York Times*

In this piece, which originally appeared in *The New York Times*, Doreen Roam gives us a glimpse of the shame, disappointment, and pain children of alcoholics feel. Sometimes children, against their best intentions, adopt their parents' worst habits and behaviors.

Father's Secret "Invisible Drinks"

It seems almost impossible that five years have passed since my father died. I often think of him as being alive. But—usually with great guilt—I consider life far easier without him.

My father was an alcoholic. In my suburb an alcoholic didn't display Bowery bum characteristics. My dad didn't drink booze out of a paper bag, and he went to work in the city every day and came home at night like other fathers. But before dinner and before changing out of his work suit, Dad would head to the kitchen cabinet where we kept the liquor. He'd pour a hefty shot of bourbon and down it, and then he'd make a drink for my mother and another for himself.

These were what I called the "visible" drinks because they were out in the open. These drinks didn't make me nervous like the "invisible" drinks—the stolen shots of liquor for which my father devised elaborate ruses to get into the kitchen. His quiet forays, he believed, were not noticed. But I knew his secret.

At home, the secret was never spoken of aloud, but it pervaded all aspects of our lives. I recall the very smell of Dad, for instance. Along with the natural masculine smells of Palmolive soap, toothpaste, and aftershave lotion was another smell I could not identify. Years later I smelled the same combination of smells on my husband after we attended a party. I told him that he smelled just like my father. Then, with the proper identification of the mystery smell, I burst into tears, knowing unmistakenly that it was gin.

There were, of course, far worse repercussions of Dad's alcoholism than the way he smelled. I, an observant child, watched his physical appearance change from that of a man as handsome as a movie star to that of a clown. His lean stomach eventually swelled up to enormous proportions and became a shelf on which he rested his crossed arms. When he still went to the beach with us, people would poke him and make fun of his belly. I watched sullenly, suffering at the knowledge that people were laughing at Dad.

I vowed a childish deadly vengeance on them all for hurting him, and for making me want to run until the shame of him I felt burning in my chest melted. Eventually he stopped coming to the beach, preferring to wander around the house, watching TV, taking naps, mailing an occasional letter.

He began to stay up at night when the rest of the house slept, claiming he suffered from insomnia. I would have believed it except for the fact that my bedroom was over the kitchen. I heard him through the night opening cabinets, clinking ice into glasses, pouring liquor out.

A few times Dad stopped drinking for a while. It was a situation almost worse than when he drank full-time. When he would stop, his personality would change, and he would become interested in the daytime and all of us around him. I prayed fervently to God not to let him want a drink. But each time he failed and returned to his old drinking habits. My hopes were dashed, and I came to believe, at the ripe age of twelve, that God was cruel to children and powerless over alcohol. I believe that still, when I think of my lost father.

In spite of the pain, I still remember some good things about Dad. He knew, for example, the name of every tree, every leaf and flower, and he had read every good book. He played the piano and could sing in a high but mellow tenor that would stop people in their tracks to listen. And very young children and animals flocked to him.

I remember one memory in particular, because it represents the way I should always like to think of Dad. Once he took us fishing at Glen Island. When my mother had too much of all eight of us children, we were split into two groups. The older children had activities with their friends in the neighborhood, but the younger children (Stephen, Michael, Mary, and I) were bundled up in sweaters on that cool blue-skied October day to hook fiddler crabs for blackfish bait.

Dad was still slim, around thirty-five; a bamboo fishing pole rested naturally in his hand, and he smoked a pipe with cherry walnut tobacco. His jet black hair contrasted with the red plaid of the jacket he wore, and standing on the rocks of the seawall he reminded me of Atticus Finch—for I had just seen the movie version of *To Kill a Mockingbird.* I hold that memory very close because after then I rarely saw that man again.

You would have to be the child of an alcoholic to really understand what it is like to deal with chaos on an everyday level. You would then also understand how a child can learn to keep a secret, or how he can learn to live with broken promises and disappointments. As the child of an alcoholic you would learn how to defend your father (or mother) to your friends, if you had any, since you would never venture to bring them home from school. You would understand the agony of how it feels to catch your parent who, thinking he is alone, belts liquor straight from the bottle. You might even understand how the child of an alcoholic can become an alcoholic himself.

I certainly do. Sadly, aware of all the warning signs of

alcoholism, and fully aware of the fact that children of alcoholics have a much greater tendency to become alcoholics than the children of nondrinkers, I developed a heavy drinking habit. Alcohol was always part of the party in our house, an overemphasized factor in any celebration. In truth, from the moment I first was allowed a glass of wine at dinner, I never learned to drink in moderation. I began to abuse alcohol.

My heavy drinking went on for six long years, until my behavior and dependence on alcohol both frightened and disgusted me. I was tired of hangovers and appalled, when I looked at a holiday photo of my family, at the way I looked. My face was puffy, and I had dark circles under my eyes; I really looked ill. It was obvious that drinking too much made me feel and look horrible, and I vowed to stop drinking.

I immediately became aware that it would be a lot tougher to stop drinking than I had thought it would be. At first it was nearly impossible to say no to a cocktail at a party or a beer at a barbecue because I had tremendous difficulty in separating alcohol from any social occasion. But somehow I persevered. I did not want to be a drunk. Instead, I wanted to break the legacy of alcoholism left by my father, to abolish the effects of drinking—like hangovers and blackouts—from my life forever. I wanted to feel good and look good, not tired and ill. I wanted my own life, not a mirror image of my dad's life. I wanted my children, when I someday had them, to be proud of me. And I grew stronger.

One year for Father's Day I made my dad an ashtray out of a handprint in clay. Another year I gave him handkerchiefs with rolled edges and some pipe cleaners. This year, though he is long gone, I still think about what I might have given to him. Perhaps it would have been some socks or a tie, an easy type of apparel gift. Yet sometimes I absolutely am convinced that this year I am giving him the best gift of all. It is the one I gave to myself:

The end of a secret, the beginning of a new life—sobriety.

MARIETTE HARTLEY

from
Breaking the Silence

Both of Mariette Hartley's parents were alcoholics, but their diseases took widely divergent paths. Her father managed to hide his drinking problem for years. Her mother's abuse of alcohol was apparent early and easily observed. Her alcoholism started as social drinking and escalated into survival drinking, turning her from a caring mother to an unresponsive automaton.

No matter how outrageous her mother's behavior, no one ever spoke about it the next day. She repeatedly attempted suicide. Throughout her childhood, Hartley believed that if she were just good enough, funny enough, or smart enough, her mother wouldn't drink.

Adding to Hartley's chaotic home life was her mother Polly's belief that children should be taught independence through an absence of any strong expression of physical affection—kissing, hugging, or touching. Polly was the daughter of behavioral psychologist John B. Watson (called Big John in the following excerpt), who promoted the theory that parents shouldn't show any strong sentiment to their children.

In later years, her mother overcame her alcoholism, but her father's worsened. Like many alcoholics, Hartley's father was suicidal and he ultimately succeeded in killing himself.

My son, Sean, got into advertising at the tender age of three, when he was in bed watching a cartoon with Patrick, cradled in the crook of Patrick's arm. Pat looked down at his young son's face, bathed in the soft glow of the television screen, and was so overtaken by a wave of emotion that he said, "Oh, Sean, I love you so much."

Without taking his eyes off the screen, Sean replied, "Thank you, PaineWebber."

Not surprising. Advertising's in his blood. My grandfather was in advertising; my husband was in advertising; even my father went into advertising.

Dad summed up his career, thencing himself through his Harvard reunion booklet:

> My first job after graduation was in the export-import business. This lasted two years. Thence a few years of skittering about, including silver fox raising in New Hampshire. I ended up in the advertising business with N. W. Ayer & Son. Thence, to BBD&O in NY. Thence, to Newell-Emmett Company and Cunningham & Walsh, after they

> absorbed the former. Thence, to retirement at sixty and into art and writing. I have painted off and on for many years, self-taught.

That's what it said in his *official biography*. In reality, after graduating in 1918, he married his first wife, hastily, and became a father, just as hastily.

He served his advertising apprenticeship at N. W. Ayer & Son in Philadelphia in the mid-twenties. Then had a brief stint as a cub with Batten, Barton, Durstine & Osborne in New York around 1930 before joining the small Madison Avenue firm of Newell-Emmett around 1934. The agency had its biggest account, Chesterfield, long before it was socially acceptable for women to smoke.

While consumers were adding halitosis, acidosis, athlete's feet, and B.O. to their list of concerns, Madison Avenue was replacing Wall Street in the minds of hotshot Ivy League grads. And the pay was excellent. A job with Young & Rubicam was instant status.

When we moved to Weston, Dad was still working for Newell-Emmett, which had been swallowed up in a spate of postwar advertising mergers by Cunningham & Walsh. Like a movie studio, an advertising agency was as good as its stable of stars. With Cunningham & Walsh, it was Texaco, Western Electric, Jaguar, the Yellow Pages, and Pepsi-Cola. Dad helped design the Pepsi script logo that was used for decades.

By now he was an account executive. I didn't know what that meant. Mom explained, "It means you have to kiss their ass. It means you have to drink with them and go on trips with them and travel back into New York after traveling from New York for dinner with them. It means you have to clean up after them, pamper them, change their diapers, and go to bed with them." From everything I know about advertising in the forties, she wasn't far from wrong. One industry definition was "Yes, sir. No, sir. Ulcer."

Returning once from a dinner with Pepsi executives, Mom was absolutely put out. "First they served us Pepsi-Cola for cocktails, then we had Pepsi-Cola for our wine drink, then we had ham basted in Pepsi-Cola. Well, I never!" (Mom would really say that, "Well, I never . . ." No one said, "Well, I never . . ." the way Mom did.) "It was the worst dinner I ever attended. They all sat around and . . . Well, I never . . ."

Dad had another account for Beech-Nut bacon with a man named Foote. Not Emerson Foote of Foote, Cone & Belding, but Simon Foote of Foote, Foote, Foote & Foote. At least that's what we called him. Fascinated by the long handles on advertising firms (Fred Allen once joked that Batten, Barton, Durstine & Osborne sounded like someone dragging a trunk down a short flight of stairs), we'd puff one cheek while hitting the t's, sending ourselves into gales of laughter with: *phfft*, *phfft*, *phfft*, and *phfft*. Simon Foote was always dragging Dad to Cuba with him. I asked Mom if they went fishing.

"Foote? He just goes drinking."

The suburbs continued to crawl outward along the train lines: Cos Cob, Riverside, away from New York at a faster pace. Advertising helped promote the image of the country gentleman. Americans went Anglo, recreating half-Tudor houses and train stations all along the eastern corridor. People dressed as if they were riding to hounds. Brooks Brothers had a run on brogues, Harris tweeds, and Wembley ties. Scarsdale resembled Stratford-on-Avon, and Larchmont looked like the Cotswolds.

"Country" clubs sprang up: golf, yacht, tennis; everyone ate club sandwiches. Dad continued his love of guns and was a founding member of the Weston Gun Club, Mom learned tennis at the Weston Field Club, and Big John rode to hounds at the Weston Hunt Club.

Developers came in to quaint it up: village greens, stone cottages; every brook had its swan. And the station wagon was exactly that. A wagon that waited at the station. In the forties came the "woodie"—the wagon with side-wood paneling. I remember fifteen to twenty woodies lined up at the train station at 5:31, waiting for dads. Each contained two children, one wife, and one dog. All of them in tweed.

Dad's drinking began a slow but steady escalation when he began the Westport–New York commute around 1946.

He started commuting the same year *The Hucksters* exploded onto the best-seller list. The talk of Madison Avenue and our dinner table, the book painted a greedy and manipulative picture of the industry. It concerned a dignified war widow, played in the movie by Deborah Kerr, huckstered into doing a testimonial for charity, shades of Big John and Pond's. The book sat on the best-seller lists for eighteen weeks while the romantic occupation took a dive.

Once a day, five days a week, Dad boarded the New York, New Haven, and Hartford. He learned to read a newspaper folded into quarters with the best of them, spending the next hour reading or dozing to the rhythms, while the conductors underlined the signs as they rolled past: "DARien! STAMford! GREENwich! MAmaroneck! LARCHmont! NEW Rochelle! GREAT Neck! Grannnnnnnd Cennntralll Staaaaaationn! Everybody off!" Debarking, he joined one of the tributaries that merged into the great hall of Grand Central Station. From there it was only a short block to Madison Avenue.

But he was born too late. He had missed the great days of the luxury railroad cars. The New York, New Haven, and Hartford had specialized in boiled Maine lobster and Cotuit oysters served in the splendor of mahogany and brass fittings. Earlier cars had indirect lighting and cooled air. By the time Dad started commuting, there was one meager fan that seldom worked, attached to the front wall of each car.

When the Connecticut Turnpike opened in 1958, the car became king, and a generation of commuters was consigned to history. Maintenance cutbacks meant that the 5:15 became the 10:52, and commuters would arrive at that Friday night dinner party in time for Saturday's breakfast. Not a total loss. There was a good chance a lot of the partygoers would still be there. Drinking.

As I look back on it, I guess Dad was pretty high every time he came home from New York. Advertising men were not only famed for their martini lunch; they were also famed for infiltrating the bar car on the infamous 5:31, the commuter special, the traveling cocktail lounge. Events in the history of the iron horse had been transposed. Long Island farmers once stoned the first locomotives; now the only things stoned were the passengers.

So Dad would arrive home slightly primed, and we'd be waiting at the station. We looked forward to having him come home from New York. My brother and I would get in our pajamas, climb into the car and sing, "Here comes my daddy now—hey pop, hey pop, hey pop." Mom would be all dressed up with that gardenia in her hair, waiting for their first drink together. Subtract the twenty minutes from the train to our house, and the cocktails would start after six. But you didn't know he was tight; he held it well. Mom was the one who didn't.

I think Mom started as a buddy drinker. I think a lot of women do. She drank with her first husband in Texas; she drank with Dad, with Big John, with the crowd. But Mom was not a good drinker, ever. Two drinks and she was over. She didn't know it, but she was.

Weston, at that time, was a hard-drinking community, and no one thought anything of it. Drinking was a part of living. Romanticized in advertising, books, and movies, getting blotto on the 5:31 was a major source of humor for *New Yorker* cartoons and Benchley briefs. "GREENwich! STAMford! SOBER UP for WESTport and SAUGAtuck!" The Algonquin Round Table of the thirties was under the table by the forties. Beer was for factory workers; wine was for dinner. The real creative artist drank martinis, manhattans, or scotch, neat.

When prohibition was over and you could buy "likker" that also tasted good, the social pendulum swung widely to the "wets." Drinking not only became acceptable; those who didn't were highly suspect. Teetotal could keep you off the party list. Especially in Weston.

For a while people drank nicely: a couple of cocktails before dinner, a little wine during, a smart liquor after. Nobody got drunk. That came later at the big weekend parties. Mom says she used to drink more at parties because they made her nervous; she thought she'd be more social. "God knows, I was social enough. I don't know why I thought I needed to get drunk. But people who didn't drink, for God's sake, were bores." She once described one of my father's many bosses: "I loved that guy; he was a good old drunk. His wife was a real alcoholic." "Good old drunk" was a sincere compliment. Trophies went to the sport who held it the most. Big John usually won. Since he loved his bourbon, he'd line his stomach with a pint of Nujol mineral oil before he went to a party. Others ate half a pound of butter.

There were a lot of artists, writers, and advertising men in Weston and Westport at that time: Robert Lawson, Hugh Lofting, Hardie Gramatky, James Daugherty, Wood Cowan, James Montgomery Flagg, Van Wyck Brooks, A. E. Hotchner, Martha Raye, Max Shulman, Johnny Held, and Fred and Ethel Mertz. (They had followed Lucy Ricardo when she moved to a television

Westport in the late fifties.) I went to school with the daughter of "This is Douglas Edwards and the News"; the Lindberghs once lived on Long Lots Road.

Mom and Dad were in the thick of this—mixing with Big John's crowd, their own crowd. They loved to entertain, and Dad was an excellent cook. I loved to see him outside by the grill with his apron on, rustling up one of his "Hishity-hash and Hell-fire Stews." They were never alike and always delicious. He made great salads, prepared steaks and roast beef beautifully, and was the best lobster chef in the world. He would charcoal-broil them—lots of butter, lots of lemon. No matter how long they stayed on the grill, they were never overcooked—another important consideration when dealing with late trains. Smart hosts knew how to stretch the cocktail hour into three.

Tony and I used to sit at the top of the stairs at our house, listening as the parties got louder and louder and more and more raucous, everyone talking of Taft and Dewey. Mom and Dad had a lot of friends, mostly couples, mostly moneyed—the Vernums, the Snaiths. Bill Snaith was the head of Raymond Loewy, a huge industrial design firm that, among other things, redesigned the famous luxury train, the "Broadway Limited," and our Studebaker.

We were hardly rich, but we were hardly poor. That

was what was so wonderful about Weston. It didn't matter whether you had a dime. If you were interesting, you were accepted. Your invitation to dinner was witty repartee. And what better way to ensure wit than by false courage? Two martinis before entrance, skip the hors d'oeuvres.

But there was no stability. Advertising men knew they could be fired if they didn't come up with the creative goods, toady to the client, or please the boss. It was common knowledge that an advertising career meant changing jobs every three or four years.

It has always fascinated me that those who need stability are the creative types, and those who live with instability are the creative types. Actors deal with it on a daily basis. I sometimes wonder if the average worker could bear to go job hunting forty or fifty times a year for the rest of his life, facing personal rejection on looks, talent, personality, reputation—earned or otherwise.

But Dad was one of the luckier ones. For fifteen years he managed to hang on at Cunningham & Walsh. Until I was nine. Until the drinking got worse.

It all turned to hell.

Throughout my early years, Dad had been a periodic drinker—weekends, nights. Sometimes when he felt it was getting out of hand, he'd even stop drinking for three weeks to a month. But it got to be fairly steady after he was fired from Famous Artists. We tried tossing his bottles in the river. That was going to be the answer.

Tony was the scapegoat more than I. At some of the high school football games, they'd reserve a special section in the stands for fathers of Staples squad members. Tony was playing; I was cheerleading. Dad would show up reeling drunk. When he had that *look*, we knew we couldn't communicate.

Tony also got the brunt of it at dinner.

"Did you mow the lawn today, Tony?"

"Yes."

"Did you pound down the mole hills? You're gonna kill the mower. Did you pound down the mole hills like I told you to?"

Mom would leap in. "Betty Snaith was in the shop today. She says Marilyn Monroe was televised on *Person to Person* from Milt Greene's. Everyone was talking about it. There must've been fifty kids standing on rock fences over on Fanton Hill Road to get a look."

Tony'd "Va-va-va-voom."

"Oh, va-va-va-voom," I'd scoff.

"Anyway, we should thank our lucky stars because I sold her two dresses. I just don't know how we're going to live if I don't do well on commissions."

Tony and I would stare at our plates.

"I've got an idea," Dad would say. "Let's write a cookbook. We'll call it *How to Cook Without a Book.*"

Mom would look at him; Dad would look down, then mumble, "Did you polish the car, Tony? Did you polish the car like I told you to?"

That spring of 1955, Dad started to paint these kind of schizophrenic, manic-depressive oils. He'd line them up outside, like an art show. God, they were awful. Some were filled with somber colors; others were filled with swirls. One had this horrible eye made of violent purple.

And the big parties were getting worse. There was always booze wherever we went: picnics, restaurants, the field club, the gun club. I brought kids home who would understand. They'd see my Dad with a buzz on and say, "Oh, hello, Mr. Hartley." Dad never had a click-off period; Mom did. Dad would just get rubbery, kind of lush and easy.

When Mom's drinking got worse, every dinner was a week long. It would start off friendly enough, especially if Mom had had a good day of commissions:

"What happened at school today, honey?"

"I got the lead in this year's musical. I'm doing everything—acting, singing, dancing, writing, producing."

"I don't know how you do it. You work so gol' darn hard."

Dad would join in. "Who else is in it?"

"Tom Winkopp, Eddie Jarman."

"Eddie Jarman?"

"He did magic tricks in the Bedford Talent Show, remember? He didn't win because the judges sat behind him and saw how he did them."

"I'm in it."

"Are you, Tony?"

"Yah, I'm in the boy's chorus line."

"Faxon's in the girl's. She's going to sing a duet with Alan Green."

"This dressing could use more lemon, don't you think?"

Mom would go to the kitchen for more lemon, but we knew better. She'd go to the kitchen for a drink; we could hear her opening the bottle. Then she'd return, we'd change our faces, and Tony'd interrupt the silence.

"Mariette made the papers."

"What papers?"

"Today's *Town Crier.*"

"Wanna hear it?"

"Sure! You get the paper, I'll get more carrots."

I'd race hell-bent for the paper—racing to beat the alcohol, racing to keep the connection. Maybe she wasn't too far gone yet, maybe if I made her laugh, maybe if I made her feel good. Because on the second drink we could hear the click. I'd look at Tony; he'd look at me; Dad would concentrate on his plate. "Say bye-bye."

Each time Mom would return there'd be a decided change. Her posture would be a little sloppier; her speech would be a little slurred. Mom cared about her appearance. She always looked soft, feminine; I can still see her fingernails, long and Revlon red. Her pride, her dignity, compounded the horror when she drank. The click was when the lipstick started to smear, and the mascara started to run. Tony and I'd just sit there, watching the decay.

I'd return with the paper and read with some urgency, hoping for a sober response before it was too late: " 'Three young stars are rising from the ranks of Staples High School. The effervescent Mariette. . .' "

Tony'd laugh, "Effervescent."

I'd counter, "Yes, effervescent."

"What's it mean?"

"Got me."

We'd all laugh, except for Mom. Her eyes would look right through us. Because we weren't us anymore, although we made the mistake of thinking we were.

She'd go back in the kitchen.

"Mom, you want to hear this!"

"Just be a minute!"

" 'The effervescent Mariette,' " I'd shout, " 'interviewed amongst her dolls yesterday, revealed her plans for a theatrical career. This beautiful redheaded "doll," '—shut up, Tony—'has studied drama for seven years. . . .' "

Dad would beam, "That's my girl."

"Mom, can you hear this?"

"I'm listening!"

" 'Sitting on a blue bedspread with a striped ruffle, Mariette told of her love for stuffed animals and dolls! A shelf across one wall of her room contains her collection, which must exceed twenty-five!' "

Mom would return.

" 'Her father, Paul Hartley, has written three books on how to paint and is now writing a Beginners Art Course.' Listen to this, Mom, listen. 'Mrs. Hartley is manager and saleswoman at the Separate Shop.' " I'd look over to Mom; there'd be a slight smile. "Did you hear that, Mom? 'Mrs. Hartley is manager and saleswoman at the Separate Shop'?"

"Does it say she wouldn't have to be if her darling husband had a job?"

"Actually no, Mom. It doesn't say that."

"Well, it should."

Dad would put down his fork. "Did you paint the fence today, Tony? Did you paint the fence like I told you to?"

It was very hard for Mom to admit the real rage. During this time her basic mood was anger—anger that she was working, anger that Dad was jobless. She was making forty bucks a week, and Dad was drinking a lot of her money away. She was tired, but the only time she let it out was after the third drink. Dad became the leech, the drunkard, the man who forced her to work.

I kept trying to figure out what was against Dad, what was against us. Ordinarily Mom had a way of speaking that was almost resigned, but when she began drinking it became a stream of vitriol. I don't think Tony and I were the targets, but the shotgun splattered.

The conversation would take an abrupt turn.

"Big John was over yesterday. He's amazed you're still out of a job. I said, 'Daddy, Paul's trying.' I didn't know what to tell him."

"There's nothing to tell."

"I don't know how you can sit around all day, Paul."

"I'm not sitting around; I'm painting."

"Um-hm, well, to each his own theory that you want to buy. I'm so proud of Daddy; they're gonna honor him in New York this fall."

Dad would get bolder, "I'm surprised they're not naming him Father of the Year."

"He was a good father!"

"I don't think Billy's particularly happy, Polly."

"That's not fair, Paul. I love my kids, but I don't believe in kissing them all over the place, I just don't. Dad's right; he just went a little overboard. I argued with him all the time about that. He loves to argue. People get wild, but they come back for advice; he gives awful good advice."

"Oh, admit it, Polly. He has a lot of crackpot theories."

"Well, at least he has some, Paul. At least he's made something of himself. Unlike some people I know. He may have gotten fired, but he didn't quit. He marched right into Madison Avenue and look what he's accomplished. That beautiful, big old house."

"Dad's trying, Mom."

"I'm going to get a job, Polly; I'm going to have a job before the week is out."

"You do that."

It was high dudgeon all night. She'd leave a room, the

door would slam, we'd wait. We knew another entrance was forthcoming, another tirade.

Dad would just sit there, muttering: "Oh, damn. Oh, goddamn. Oh, God."

It got so that every night we'd sit down to dinner and it would start. Like the Chinese water torture, the same thing all over again—the same arguments, the same accusations, the same door slams. Then we'd wake up the next day with so many questions that we didn't dare ask. There was a fragility in the house, a feeling of walking on eggs. We could never criticize.

And since Mom had blackouts, she never remembered. I'd wake the next morning, and it was, "Hi, how are you? Is everything fine?" It was chilling. I wanted to ask, "Did you know I found you in the bushes?" But I didn't know how to say it so she wouldn't feel ashamed. When you wake up and everything's business as usual, it tests your sanity. You can't ask, "Do you remember last night? Do you remember the pain you caused Dad, you caused Tony, you caused me? I really don't want to go through a night like that again."

I started drinking with Sandy when I was fourteen; we'd go to his house or across the state line. He was a much better drinker than I. I was more like my mother. I didn't know where I was, what I was doing, or who he was.

We were also making love.

It didn't have much to do with sex; it had a lot to do with needing to be held. But I was not ready for sex at fourteen; it had so many other implications. Everything got to be too close, too tight, so I'd pull away. I remember once throwing rocks at him on the football field. The only way I could deal with the pressures was to hit out at him.

Drinking made me a lot more free sexually; the restrictions were off. I was a compulsive, compliant "good girl" by day and a "bad girl" at night. I know now I wasn't a bad kid. I didn't know it then.

I felt like a hypocrite. Standing there in the choir of the Norfield Congregational Church, singing solos. By now, I was a very popular kid. I was an honor student; I had accumulated a stack of yearbook credits: "Most Popular, Best Disposition, Best Personality," and, ironically, the "Good Citizenship" medal. I was a cheerleader, standing at the games in front of the bleachers, in front of everybody, knowing that I was evil, knowing they could all see it. I wasn't wearing a megaphone; I was wearing Hester's *A.* I think that was the reason for the compulsion; I was afraid they would see the other side, the dark side. Even though I knew someday Sandy and I would get married, I felt like a whore.

I once confided in Marcia Cassedy. Not the smartest move—I picked a staunch Catholic. I should have picked a short atheist. She told me if I had sex again, if I didn't ask for forgiveness, I'd go to hell. (Marcia Cassedy is now a psychotherapist living in Palos Verdes.)

I felt strange. I remember coming into Mom's room one morning. "Mom, I keep thinking in the past tense. I keep thinking about this girl that was."

About six months ago I dreamt I was on a sandy beach with the sun beating down, permeating my body. Then a shadow came between me and the sun. It was a huge bird, like an eagle, but dangerous, like a griffin—wings spread, coming toward me. It landed on my stomach. It had talons, red, bloody talons, that ripped open my skin, split open my stomach. I tried to get away from it. I ran through a wood toward a small cabin, threw open the door, and looked behind. It hadn't followed me; I was away from it. So I slammed the door shut. When I turned, it was standing next to me. I hadn't seen it come in. But it was there.

SUZANNE SOMERS

from
Keeping Secrets

Although her alcoholic father's midnight tirades hindered her schoolwork and social life, Somers never let on that her family lived in terror of this bully. Neither did her two brothers, her sister, or her mother. In fact, few neighbors ever realized that the family inside the neat house with the manicured lawn was any different from their own. Somers and her family made sure the father made it to his job at the brewery every day, a job where he had ready access to all the beer he could drink.

Although she never became an alcoholic herself, Somers did adopt the life-style of crisis. She married at seventeen when she was pregnant, then ended the marriage within a year, facing motherhood alone.

She eventually found success in the TV sitcoms *Three's Company*, *She's the Sheriff*, and *Step by Step* as well as Las Vegas nightclubs and hotels.

In 1990 Somers, who often speaks to groups of adult children of alcoholics, founded the Suzanne Somers Institute for the Effects of Addictions on the Family, a Palm Springs referral service that also sets up programs in hospitals and treatment centers.

"Be quiet, for Godsakes," my mother pleaded.

"Oh, fuck you," Dad yelled drunkenly. "Your ol' man ain't nothin'! Goddamn leech! Gobbles everything in two minutes. I could beat the shit outa him. The pig! Two kind words—ass and hole. Zero! Big nothin'!"

"Shut up," my mother screamed.

"Tell your ol' man he's nothin," Dad slurred. "I could take him."

"Sure, you could beat up an old man. Would that make you feel good?" she asked angrily.

I was nine years old. I lay in my bed listening to the same old drunk talk night after night. Well, some nights Dad would pass out and sleep through; but on other nights, usually when he was drinking lots of whiskey, he might sleep for four hours or so; and then he'd wake up belligerent—ready to fight anyone. Somehow, someone would become the victim of his rage. Often it was my grandfather, whom we called Father. I guess that ticked him off. Sometimes his rage would be aimed at me because I made it very clear I liked my mother better. Some nights, for no reason in particular, it would be Danny, my thirteen-year-old brother, or Maureen, my sixteen-year-old sister, who set him off. Maybe Danny didn't mow the lawn just right, or Maureen wore lipstick. You never knew. He'd just get full of "stinkin' thinkin' " and one little thing would set him off all night.

"Can I get into bed with you?" my mother asked me. "He's starting to shadowbox in bed, and I don't want a black eye."

I loved my mother so much. It made me hate my father when he'd do this to her. It was four o'clock in the morning. Mom would have to go to work at nine A.M. Maureen, Danny, and I all had school at eight A.M. None of us would have had any sleep. It had been one of the "terrible nights." Dad came home from work drunk. Sometimes he would start drinking after he got home, but the nights he came home from work already drunk were the worst—like tonight. He had stumbled in the front door earlier this evening and saw Father sitting in the living room, reading the paper. That set him off. He was jealous of Father and resented his being "at home" in our house. I loved Father and felt very protective of him when Dad started in on him.

Mom had quickly called us all to dinner. She was nervous and figured if she got food into Dad, he might feel better, or best yet, fall asleep. Of course, we all "knew" he wouldn't eat food or fall asleep when he was like this. We sat down at our places at the table.

"Where'd you get this meat?" Dad yelled. "Your ol' man bring this shit?" Tension.

"Yes," said Father. "They were going to throw it out at the butcher shop, so I took it and told Marion [my mother, his daughter] to marinate it in a little vinegar for a while and it would be just fine."

"Why don'cha tell your ol' man we don't need his old meat around here!" he yelled drunkenly to my mother.

"Pass the potatoes, please," I said. I hated when dinners started like this. Maybe I could change the subject of meat. Actually, I hated the meat, too. It smelled, and I wished Father wouldn't bring it.

Father was a product of the Depression and couldn't waste anything. When they were cleaning up at the butcher shop at the end of the day, he would take the meat or fish that couldn't be sold anymore because of the smell and the color, and he would bring it to my mother. It was hard to say anything to him about it because his intentions were so sweet. My mother didn't want to hurt his feelings.

Father was getting older now, about seventy-five, and needed to feel he was contributing. He ate dinner with us three times a week. The other four days he divided his time between my Aunt Helen's and Uncle Ralph's—my mother's sister and brother.

"Danny, don't eat all the potatoes. There are five of us, you know," I said. I loved potatoes. I practically lived on them because of the meat. I usually ate just potatoes and salad. "Pass the butter, please," I said. I also loved butter.

Dad watched the butter pass from Danny to Maureen to me. He watched my knife go into the butter. I knew he was going to make butter an issue this meal, so I deliberately took a teeny bit. Ha, ha. There's nothing he can say. Using too much butter could send him into a crazy rage.

"Danny, go in the garage and get me a beer," Dad said.

"Eat some dinner first," Mom said nervously.

"I don't want this shit! Old rancid meat! Your father thinks he's a big man bringing this shit! Know what I think about this *shit*? Huh? *Nothin'*!" He threw his chop at the kitchen door.

"Stop it," Mom shouted.

"Oh, why do you have to be this way?" Father asked painfully.

"You know why?" Dad screamed. "You wanna know why? Because I've got assholes like you leeching off me every night."

"I'm not here every night," Father said.

"My ass, you're not."

"You want me to leave?" Father asked.

"Yeah! Get the fuck outa here," Dad yelled.

"No, Father! Please don't go!" I cried.

Mom got up and ran from the table crying. Danny sat at the table seething. You could tell he wanted to kill Dad; Maureen's eyes filled with tears. I hated Daddy. He ruined everything. Father walked to the living room. I followed him.

"Please don't go, Father," I said. "We love you. We want you to come here. I wish you lived with us all the time. I wish he'd go away and you would be our father."

"I think if I leave now, he might calm down," Father said. He was shaking. "Your dad's in one of 'those moods' tonight, and I think looking at me is not going to make him any better."

I walked Father to the door. I felt so bad when Dad treated him like this. He lived alone, and I knew he went home only to sleep. He could probably go over to Auntie Helen's for coffee right now, I thought.

When I returned to the kitchen, Maureen and Danny were clearing the table of half-eaten food. Dad was still sitting at the table drinking his beer. He never left his beer. He also knew where my mother hid all his "bottles" (that meant whiskey). He had probably found the one in the laundry hamper because he was starting to get that real mean look in his eye. "If we all get the dishes done perfectly, then he won't be able to get crazy mad at us," I thought nervously. Maureen washed, Danny dried, and I put away. Usually Danny would use the dish towel to whip me. He would twist up the wet towel and snap it at me. I would scream and cry and yell at anyone who would listen, "Danny's hurting me." It was a great way to get attention. But tonight we'd do none of this. We all knew. Do the dishes quietly and then sneak off to our rooms and hope he'd leave us alone.

Dad walked from the dinner table to the refrigerator. Oh, no, he's really looking tonight, I thought.

"What's this?" he yelled. "Two peas in a dish!" He threw the dish across the kitchen. *Crash!* "Look at this. Some old salad." He threw it at the cabinet. The sound of breaking glass brought my mother running in.

"Oh, stop this," she screamed.

"I hate the way you keep the refrigerator," he yelled drunkenly. With that, he started throwing everything he saw in the refrigerator. Suddenly milk was on the floor, smashed eggs, broken dishes with leftovers.

Danny couldn't stand it. He leaped on Dad, punching him, trying to throw him on the floor. Dad was drunk so he went down easily.

"You cocksucker," Dad yelled.

"Stop it, Danny. You'll get hurt," Mom screamed.

"Stop it," I cried.

Maureen watched icily. I could tell she couldn't wait to move out of this house.

For the moment it was over.

"You better go stay at the Mullinses' house tonight," Mom whispered to Danny. She knew that later Danny would be Dad's target.

I was trembling. I hated these evenings. It was always the same. I clung to my mother. She was shaking. We both started to clean up the mess of broken dishes and food.

Dad sat and watched us—looking mean. The night wasn't over. This was a whiskey night. Sometimes on whiskey nights he wouldn't fall asleep till the sun was rising.

Maureen must have called Bill, her boyfriend, because he came by and Maureen went out.

Mom and I finished cleaning up the mess. Mom cut her hand on one of the broken dishes. She ran cold water over it. I could see that her hands were trembling.

"Let's go to Shaw's and get an ice cream," Mom said. Her eyes looked tired.

I loved ice cream, but right now I would welcome any excuse to get out of this house. We left. We hoped that when we returned, Dad would be asleep.

Mom and I got our ice cream and then stopped by Auntie Helen's. We were killing time. Father was there having coffee. We didn't mention to him what had happened after he left. It would only upset him more. We told him Dad was asleep. He could relax now. Tomorrow would be a better day.

We got home around nine-thirty P.M. Maureen was still out with Bill. Dad was asleep, sitting up at the kitchen table. His legs were wrapped around each other. His cigarette in one hand had completely burned out; probably burned his finger, but he couldn't feel a thing. His other hand was wrapped around his beer. Maybe he'll just stay here all night, we hoped. Mother and I tiptoed past him and quietly got ourselves ready for bed. I got under the covers and prayed that when he awakened, he would quietly get into bed and sleep the rest of the night. Mother didn't kiss me good-night. She was lost in her own thoughts.

The sound of Dad's stumbling woke me up. Maybe he'll go right to bed, I prayed.

"Where's Danny?" I heard him yell. "Where the fuck is he?"

Suddenly, the overhead lights flipped on in our bedroom. Maureen and I sat bolt upright in our twin beds. My mother came running in.

"Get out of here. Let them sleep. Some people sleep, you know!" she shouted.

With that, he sat at the foot of my bed, slightly on the edge of my feet, pulling the covers so tight I couldn't move my feet.

"You like Mommy?" he said. "I like Mommy."

Oh, God, I thought. This again. He'd slip in and out of moods. From rage to sloppy, lovey-dovey. It made me so nervous. I never knew what to expect.

"Oh, would you come to bed?" my mother said angrily, and pulled him off the end of my bed. She understood this mood. He wasn't violent now; just drunk, insensitive, and obnoxious. She pushed and pulled him down the hall.

He kept saying "bullshit."

Six A.M. The alarm rang. I felt so worn out. My mother was already up. Oh, God, I wet the bed. I didn't know why I couldn't stop. If anyone at school knew, I'd die. Sandy knew (she was my best friend), although Sandy didn't know that I did it every night. I opened the window and pushed the mattress outside to dry. I put the wet sheets in the wash and wiped clean the rubber sheet. Dad came out of the bathroom. I waited in my room till I was sure he was in the kitchen. I didn't want to see him. He was always real edgy in the morning, and he was probably still a little drunk. I'm sure he didn't feel very good. All that whiskey and beer and no food.

My sister dashed past me and locked herself in the bathroom.

"Hurry in there," I said. "I'm all wet." My pajamas smelled and stuck to me. It was cold.

My dad walked by. "Wet the bed again, pisshead?" he said.

I hated him. I wished he would go away and never come back.

"Maure-e-en! Hurry up. I have to go to school, too! Mom, tell Maureen to get out."

"Quit whining," Dad said. He smelled like stale beer. He went into the garage, and I heard the engine start. "Thank God, he's gone."

I took a bath in two inches of water. It took too much time to fill the tub in the morning; and besides, five people had to share the hot water and one bathroom.

"Suzanne, come eat your oats!" Mom called from the kitchen.

I finished putting on my uniform and sat down at the breakfast table.

"It's Wednesday, so I'll be going grocery shopping after work," my mother said. "Do you want to come?"

I loved to go grocery shopping with her on payday. That way I could get her to buy my favorites—mortadella and cheese, sourdough French bread, and Hostess

Twinkies. Lunches on Thursday were always great. By Friday all the food would be gone because Danny always made himself three or four sandwiches after dinner. "Yes! I want to go with you," I said. "I'll come home right after school." When the bell rang at three o'clock that afternoon, I skipped home eagerly.

Mom and I returned from shopping around 5:30. No one was home. We never mentioned last night. We didn't want to acknowledge what had happened; maybe then it would go away. Above all, we knew never to let anyone outside our home know the truth. It was too shameful, too embarrassing, too crazy.

There was a note on the kitchen table from Father saying he wouldn't be able to stay for dinner tonight. He was a widower, and his girlfriend had asked him out. (His girlfriend, Mrs. Miller, was sixty-five years old.)

Mom and I didn't say anything to each other, but I felt relieved that Father wouldn't be here. If Dad wasn't home by this time, it wasn't good news. He started out this morning still a little drunk (and *not* in a good mood), so he'd probably been drinking all day to take the edge off his hangover. Dad had the worst job in the world for someone who liked to drink a lot. He loaded cases of beer onto boxcars at Lucky Lager Brewery. For every few cases of beer he put onto the train, he took one beer for himself. After eight hours of this, he would get pretty "looped."

It was so peaceful when he wasn't home. Maureen and Danny came home just before dinner. Even so, there was a tension in the air. Every time we heard a noise while eating, we would all look up wondering if that was the garage door. But so far tonight we were lucky. (Or were we?)

I went to my room to do my homework. I didn't have my homework finished at school today, and I got into trouble again from Sister Cecile. I was in the fourth grade at our parish Catholic school.

I never had my schoolwork done. It was impossible to study and do homework at home. We couldn't ignore Dad when he was drunk, and he was drunk most nights. He demanded our attention. He followed us around the house either in a rage or rambling unintelligible mumblings. His mumblings were full of questions though, and he demanded that they be answered.

Usually, "Do you love Mommy? Huh? Mommy doesn't love me! Why doesn't Mommy love me? Huh? Huh? Huh?"

Finally, we'd answer in exasperation and a shrill voice, "Because you drink too much!"

Then the anger would start. "Bullshit!" he'd yell back.

We all knew it was stupid to talk to him when he was like this, but we allowed ourselves to be pushed into it. We had the disease. We were addicted to the alcoholic. This went on night after night. Who could think about school? School was just a place to go to get out of the house. My thoughts were never far away from the problems at home. I had already accepted the fact that I wasn't very smart. That's why I didn't get good grades. But in reality, how could I get good grades when all my energies and attention were directed toward the craziness at home? Our disease was our priority. We perpetuated our disease, night after night. I never thought about school until I was at school, and then it was too late.

I got ready for bed and went to find my mother to say good-night. She was sitting in the dark, in the breakfast room, smoking a cigarette. That was her big vice. She was still the "good girl"—forty years old and hiding her smoking from her father. He never came around this late at night anyway, but she could deal with it better hiding in the dark, in the back of the house.

"Good-night, Mommy. I love you," I said.

"Good-night, honey," she said. I noticed her hands were shaking holding the cigarette. "I love you, too, sweetheart."

I lingered for a moment. Sometimes I needed more

from my mother than she could give me. It wasn't that she wouldn't give me what I needed emotionally, nor was it that she couldn't; but the disease had turned all her energies inward trying to cope. Mother was in so much pain herself, she couldn't know the pain I was in. She felt guilty, she felt sorry for all of us, and dealt with it by praying. She prayed for God to help her husband.

I awoke from a deep sleep at the sound of the doorbell ringing loudly and incessantly.

"Do you have to wake up the whole house?" I heard my mom yell in a whisper.

I looked at my clock. It was midnight.

"It's my fuckin' house, and I can do whatever I want!" he yelled.

"Watch out, you're going to knock over the table," my mother shouted.

"Why? Did your father give us the fuckin' table? Big man! He gives you four hundred dollars every Christmas and a bunch of rancid meat!" he slurred.

It was going to be a belligerent night. I started to cry. It scared me and made me so nervous when he was like this. I was so afraid he'd hurt my mother. He wouldn't hurt her on purpose; but when she was trying to pick him up or get him into bed, he'd throw punches into the air and sometimes he'd connect. He was really drunk tonight. I could hardly understand anything he was saying. He wasn't making any sense. Just a lot of bad words seemed to come out clearly. Mom got Dad into the bedroom and closed the door. I could hear his muffled drunk sounds and my mother's suppressed shouting.

"Would you shut your mouth," Mom said angrily. She was exasperated and tired.

"I will not!" he answered drunkenly.

All of a sudden their door opened. Oh, no, I thought. He's going to come in here. Maybe I'll hide in the closet. My dad stumbled into the bathroom. "Thank God," I thought. Maybe he'll just pee and then go to sleep. Through the wall I could hear him peeing. Then some more stumbling. He didn't flush the toilet. All of a sudden the overhead light flipped on in our bedroom.

"Where's Maureen?" he shouted. He went over and sat down on Maureen's feet. "You're gonna get knocked up," he said to Maureen. "I know what that Kilmartin wants, the big galoot!" Kilmartin was what he called Maureen's boyfriend, Bill Gilmartin. He was jealous of Bill because he was big—six feet tall, two hundred pounds; and, also, because he was taking out Maureen. Dad didn't like anyone who wanted to go out with Maureen, especially big ones. My dad is a little guy. He must have hated being small because he talked about it a lot when he was drunk.

"Would you get out of here and shut up!" Maureen shouted.

My mother came running in. "Get out of here! Leave them alone!" she said. She started pulling him off the bed.

"I will not!" he shouted. He pushed her away. He was strong. She landed on the floor.

"Stop it!" I screamed. I couldn't stand to see my mother hurt. Mother started crying.

"You're crazy!" Maureen shouted. She stood up and tried to push him off the bed.

I got on the floor to keep my father away from my mother. He was swearing. Maureen was screaming. My mother was crying. I was sobbing. Danny came running downstairs.

"You asshole," Danny screamed.

"Don't, Danny. You'll only make things worse," my mother said desperately. "I'll get him in bed," she said. She dragged my father down the hall. He stumbled and swore and punched at the air.

I lay in bed and listened to him swearing and cussing at the darkness for a long, long time. I couldn't stop shaking and crying. Maureen was crying, also. I suspected everyone in the house was crying. Except him.

Ring! The alarm went off. I jumped. Morning already. I felt like I hadn't had any sleep at all. I didn't hear any noise in the house. I walked into the living room. My mom was asleep, huddled in the corner of the couch with her coat thrown over her shoulder. I often found her sleeping on the couch. It didn't seem abnormal. I understood why she was afraid to sleep with him. He kicked, yelled, and punched at the air.

"Daddy's not up yet, Mom. He's gonna be late for work," I said. My dad never missed work, no matter how drunk he'd been the night before. I got some stability out of that. If he could make it to work every day, then he wasn't all that bad. Missing work meant he really was a drunk and, also, we'd be poor. There would be no food, and someone might come and take our house away. I worried a lot. Mom got off the couch and went to the bedroom.

"Holy shit," I heard him say. He sounded like he was still drunk. He sounded mean. "Get my lunch ready," he demanded. He slammed the bathroom door. I heard him coughing up terrible things and making awful noises with his nose. He slammed open the bathroom door, got dressed, and went into the garage. Ah, peace, I thought. *Slam!* "Where the fuck is my car?" he ranted. "Did Danny steal my fuckin' car?" Danny was only thirteen years old. How could he take the car?

"How should I know where it is. Where did

you leave it?" my mother asked angrily.

His drunkenness made him do stupid things like lose the car. Dad never remembered anything about the night before. He knew we were all mad at him, so he used reverse psychology. He turned it all around. Now he was mad at us! Somehow in his twisted, wet brain *we* had wronged him. Now he could justify yelling at us and ordering my mother around. It also justified the drinking he would be doing during this day.

"I musta left it at Newell's Bar. Drive me down there," he ordered.

My mother grudgingly ran to get the keys to her '50 Chevy. Then they were gone. I grabbed a Twinkie and some chocolate milk for breakfast.

Danny came into the kitchen. "He's such an asshole," Danny said.

"I hate him," I said.

Maureen came in and said, "I can't wait till I get married and get out of here." She was so lucky. She was a senior in high school. At the end of this year she could get a job, get married, leave home, do whatever she wanted. It seemed like I'd never get out of that house.

There was nothing more to say to each other. It had been a typical night in a typical week of our lives. The pattern was firmly established.

I woke up with a start. I didn't know where I was. Then I realized that everyone in the class was laughing at me. Sister Cecile was standing over my desk. "Miss Mahoney, what *is* the capital of Montana?" I couldn't think. How long had I been sleeping? "Maybe we should talk to the principal about why you can't stay awake in class. Don't your parents make sure you go to bed on time?" she questioned. If only she knew the truth.

I was so tired from the night before, but I couldn't tell her that. It was my secret. I couldn't let anyone know my secret. How could I tell her that we were up all night with screaming and yelling and hitting? How could I tell her I finally cried myself to sleep at five A.M.? How could I tell her how nervous I was? How could I tell her this was a normal part of my life; that most nights were like this?

No teacher ever asked me if there was something wrong. They just assumed I was one of those lazy students. I'm not even sure if they *had* asked what I would have said. I was already, at nine years old, used to covering up; pretending that life inside our house was as pretty as the outside. Any house with a front lawn that perfect must house a perfect family. How could I tell anyone, "I don't know what normal is. I go to sleep on time, but night after night I'm awakened by my father's drunkenness and violence. I hide in my closet most nights. I never know what's going to happen. I'm scared. I'm sad, and I need help."

"I'm sorry," I said. "I'll go to bed early from now on." I always felt so stupid in class. I never connected my so-called stupidity to our alcoholism. I blamed myself. I had a hard time concentrating. I'd try to do my schoolwork, but I just couldn't think. I daydreamed a lot. I fantasized. I'd dream of something wonderful like being a big star on Broadway, and my mother would be sitting in the front row so proud and happy. Or I'd daydream that Debbie Reynolds and Eddie Fisher had car trouble, and they came to our house to use our phone, and we invited them to stay for dinner, and they just loved us (especially me), and my dad would be so funny and fun. The life of the party.

At three P.M. the school bell rang. School was out. Thank goodness. Instead of school being a place to escape the trauma of my home life, it became another kind of prison. I was dumb and stupid in school. I hid from my dad at home, and I hid from my teacher at school. I always tried to sit at the back of the room, out of Sister Cecile's eyesight. I would panic when she called my name. I was never paying attention. The kids in my class made fun of me. I wasn't smart and I was skinny. Boney Mahoney they called me. I had big blue eyes, long eyelashes, and chin-length blondish-brown hair that my mother combed into a pageboy. She told me I had beautiful hair. "It's so thick and shiny," she'd say. I always wore a belt to keep my uniform skirt from falling right off my waist. I wasn't "in" with the popular kids. Sandy was my only friend. She seemed to understand me; and when she saw my dad drunk, she didn't ask any questions. Even so, I avoided having her come to my house too often. Her dad drank also, but not as much as mine. Sandy and I looked alike—both blond, short, and skinny. We were best friends. We lived about a half hour's walk from one another, so we weren't able to play together every day; but we hung out at school. Sometimes, on weekends, I'd stay overnight at her house, but my fear of wetting the bed prevented me from staying too often. When I did stay, I didn't sleep well. I'd try to keep awake to make sure I wouldn't pee; but after hours of trying, I'd get so exhausted I'd fall into a deep sleep. It was always then that my bladder let loose. It would be so embarrassing the next morning. I didn't want Sandy to know, but there was no way to cover it up.

I skipped home from school one afternoon and changed out of my uniform. After grabbing my roller skates, I went out to play. My neighbors, Janie and Johnnie, were on the sidewalk in front of my house, so I started to skate with them. We tied our sweaters around our waists and held on to each other and played whip. It was so much fun. I didn't like being the tail, though; it was too scary. About five o'clock I saw our green Chevy coming down Cypress Avenue. I hoped Janie and Johnnie wouldn't notice my dad. I hoped he wasn't drunk. I felt so nervous. As the car got closer, I could see it swerve down the hill. Dad made a left-hand turn onto Crystal Springs Road. He ran over two corners. For a minute I thought he was going to do a complete circle at the intersection, but at the last moment he straightened out the wheel and proceeded left on Crystal Springs Road. He turned left again into our driveway, sideswiped the oak tree, and scraped against the picket fence. He didn't put the car in the garage. Instead, he rolled out of the passenger seat (he couldn't get out of the driver's seat because the fence was in the way) and stumbled to the front gate. The gate would stick onto the concrete front path, so to open it, you had to lift it up. In Dad's drunken state he forgot and leaned over to open the latch from the inside; he lost his balance and fell over the top of the gate. There he was, impaled on the pickets, legs and arms waving drunkenly. I was mortified. Janie, Johnnie, and I all acted like we didn't see him. I suggested maniacally that we go skate up the hill.

An hour later it was dark. If I didn't get home, my mother would be worried.

When I reluctantly walked in the back door, I knew it was not good. Dinner wasn't ready, the table wasn't set. No one was around.

Then I heard my mother yelling, "I hate this. I can't stand it anymore! I'm going to get a divorce!"

Oh, please don't get a divorce, I thought. He isn't that bad. Even the thought of divorce at that time was awful. I didn't know anyone whose parents were divorced. How could we live? I felt so scared. So terrified. What would happen to our family?

I heard my dad laugh. "You're not going to leave me, Mommy," he said drunkenly. He was right. "Mommy" threatened divorce a lot, but she never went through with it.

I ran into their room. "Please, please don't divorce him, Mommy. I love Daddy. I want us all to be together. Please!" I started crying.

My dad called me over. He was drunk, but it was a lovey-dovey, mellow drunk. He was probably exhausted. All of us were, and our nerves were raw.

"Mommy wants to leave me. Do you think she should leave me? Huh, Suzanne? I love Mommy," he said. "Isn't Mommy great?" Dad loved Mother a lot and said it over and over when he was drunk. He thought she was a saint. Deep down I'm sure he was terrified that she'd leave him.

"Yeah. Well you sure have a funny way of showing your love," my mother said angrily.

"Don't talk to him that way, Mommy." I was so afraid they'd break up. I just wanted everything to be nice and happy. A perfect family.

"Well, he's driving me crazy. I just want to get out of here forever!" my mother screamed.

"No, no. Please don't leave him," I cried. "I'll be so good. I'll never do anything wrong ever again; just please stay together."

My father lit a cigarette, took a swig of beer with the other hand and started mumbling unintelligibly. He was almost asleep. Mom and I went to the kitchen. I set the table and made the salad dressing. Mom made hamburgers, lost in her thoughts. Danny and Maureen came home. We sat down to eat.

Suddenly, Dad started yelling from the bedroom, "Shit! Fuck!"

We all ran to him. Dad had fallen asleep with the lighted cigarette and started a small fire. He had burned his finger, and the mattress was smoking. Dad poured the rest of his beer into the smoking hole in the bed. The sickly smell of beer and smoke filled the room.

"See what you do! I can't stand it! I can't stand it!"

she screamed hysterically. "Get your things, all of you. We're leaving! Now." She didn't lose it like this very often, so we knew she meant for us to get our things. I grabbed my uniform and my pajamas and got into the car. Maureen and Danny got into the backseat.

"Where're we going?" I asked.

"To a motel till I know what to do," my mother said. She was trembling.

I felt so scared and so sad. We were going to be the first divorced family in San Bruno. We went to the El Rancho Motel. The clerk asked my mother for her credit card.

"I don't have any credit cards," she said wearily.

"I'm sorry, ma'am. You can't check in without a credit card."

Mother felt so helpless. The one time she tried to break out, the one time she mustered the courage to try to save her dying family, she was stopped. She couldn't function financially on her own.

We all piled back into the car. My mother just sat at the steering wheel and started crying. It was nine o'clock. There was nothing to do but to go back home.

Dad was in bed, talking in his sleep; the usual "cocksucker, asshole," etc. Mom got into bed with me, and we both immediately fell into an exhausted sleep.

At six A.M. the following morning our door slammed

open. "Rise and shine for the dollar line!" my dad belligerently yelled at the top of his lungs. He flipped on the overhead light. "Get out-a bed, you lazy slobs." This was the semisober general. He was feeling righteous and angry for having slept alone. "Well, isn't this cute," he said. "All the girls in one room; and there's Mommy with her little favorite."

I couldn't move because I had wet the bed and didn't want him to know. Dad loved to yell at me for wetting the bed. My mother got out of bed. She didn't say anything about me peeing all over her.

Mom went to church that morning as she almost always did. It was part of her daily routine. Mass before work, always praying to God to make life like it used to be. She didn't want more, she just wanted the love and laughter that she once had back in her life. She wanted to keep the family together; she wanted the terror and sadness to be gone from her children's eyes. There was no other place to turn. She prayed for it to be God's will.

JOYCE MAYNARD

from
Parenting

Joyce Maynard, a columnist for *Parenting* magazine, says, "I write about my life because it's what I have the most intimate knowledge of." Her experiences have broad appeal and speak to the needs of many readers. She is one of the magazine's most popular feature writers. Maynard is the prolific author of several books, a syndicated column, newspaper and magazine articles, and TV scriptwriting. She lives with her children in Keene, New Hampshire. In this column she shares how her own experience as the child of an alcoholic parent shapes her parenting style.

Truth to Tell

I've written about my life and my family's life for so long that people often ask me how I can reveal so much about myself so freely. My answer is always the same: Telling a painful truth can be scary, but keeping it secret is infinitely more frightening. This is especially true when it comes to being honest with children.

So I have a very simple rule. I tell my kids the truth, which is not the same as telling them everything. In addition to believing in talking frankly about difficult subjects, I feel that it's important for parents to steer clear of even seemingly innocuous deception and avoidance of the truth. Tell a child a lie, and you teach her to lie. Avoid an uncomfortable subject altogether, and you teach her something at least as damaging: that her pain or fear is shameful and must be endured alone. You do something else, as well. You enlist her as a conspirator in your own discomfort. I know, because that's what happened to me when I was a little girl.

I grew up in an alcoholic household. But as difficult

as it was dealing with my father's drinking, the greater pain for me was the secret keeping. Adult children of alcoholics refer to the phenomenon as "the elephant in the living room": You have a huge, inescapable fact about your life that affects everything in your home, but nobody mentions it, although everybody's behavior is altered to accommodate or deal with it.

Our family squeezed past the elephant in the living room, felt his breath on our faces, and rearranged the furniture to make room for him. I hid liquor bottles if a friend was coming over. To prevent my father from driving, I even stashed away the keys to his car. But I never uttered a word, and neither did the rest of my family, about what was behind those actions.

Even if we had spoken about my father's drinking, I doubt we could have done anything to change or end it. But certainly, if all the energy we put into concealing the problem had gone instead toward addressing it, we could have at least helped each other deal with it and given each other support and strength. Instead of isolating ourselves, we might have found some measure of comfort in the world outside our home.

It wasn't until I became an adult myself that I recognized the unhealthiness of our family's conspiracy of silence—a realization that has been responsible for my decision to operate differently with my own children and friends. My childhood taught me that no demon is as terrifying as the one you don't see, the one you imagine in the dark, under your bed. Best of all, of course, would be to live one's life without demons, but knowing how unlikely that is, I've chosen to turn the lights on and talk about the demons instead.

Today, if something especially upsetting or painful is going on in our family, I name it and then talk about it. If one of my children asks me a question, I try to answer it directly, whether he wants to know "What's that funny-looking thing lying on the sidewalk?" (answer: a condom) or "Did you ever take any drugs?" (yes, and I didn't like the way they made me feel).

This kind of openness isn't right for everyone. The nineties are a different era from the one in which I grew up. Even though Oprah can talk about the sexual abuse in her past on national television, and a former First Lady can now admit to substance-abuse problems, most of us maintain a surprising degree of secretiveness about our lives. We may tell our children we want them to be open, to confide in us, but we're a lot less likely to be honest with them about our own problems.

I think it was the experience of speaking openly with my mother about her diagnosis of terminal cancer four years ago and finally confronting the years of concealment and deception in our family that allowed me to face problems in my own household that I'd tried to bury. For years, I had stayed in a tense marriage out of a belief that our children would be irreparably scarred by divorce. And so—I now understand—they had silently observed our unhappiness and were well on the way to learning the lesson of my own childhood: Pretend things are OK when they aren't.

When my marriage ended, I knew there was nothing to be gained (and plenty to be lost) by airing my grievances toward their father. No child needs to hear those things in the interests of some twisted idea of honesty or openness. By the same token, they understood that something large and painful was happening in all of our lives. I knew I couldn't shield them from the upheaval, grief, and fear of the unknown. I could, however, convey to them my willingness to communicate about the divorce.

Not that they necessarily wanted to. I don't think there are many children who immediately feel comfortable talking about real-life pain. Often I'll say things in the safety of our car at night, with my hands on the steering wheel and my eyes fixed firmly on the road. My children learned most of what they know about puberty and menstruation in our old Ford station wagon, and about the impending death, from AIDS, of a beloved family friend. The car was also where my sons have told me some of their own most troubling feelings.

Because I pick the kids up from their father's house on Sunday nights, the car is also where a lot of their decompression about our divorce takes place. Sometimes I may simply say nothing more than "Sunday nights are hard, aren't they?" They may not respond, but I know they hear me.

Two years after our divorce, my former husband and I entered into a legal battle for custody of our children, launching us all into the excruciating process of being evaluated by a court-appointed guardian. I wished that our children could have been spared the ordeal, but unable to protect them from that, I struggled with ways to explain what was going on. The truth of what was happening seemed too hard to discuss. So I chose, at first, to avoid it.

Now, looking back at that period, I wonder why I hesitated to speak. The children knew that the two people they loved more than anybody else on earth were angry at each other and that we were experiencing grave financial strain. They certainly knew that I was worried and unhappy, and they must have seen the same emotions in their father.

It took a while, but I finally asked myself, "What did we really have to hide?" The children hadn't done anything wrong. I didn't feel I had either. So why couldn't we talk about it?

In an odd way, I think the person I was protecting by not talking about the custody battle was not myself, or my children, but their father, who had initiated this action without telling the children. He had, in effect, tacitly laid down the ground rules for all of us to follow, conveying the message that painful situations are unmentionable.

In the end, I rejected that way of dealing with our children. And I know now that I will always choose to be open and communicative not only about the successes in our lives, but also about the darker, scarier parts. I don't seek to unburden my problems on my children—that's what friends and therapists are for. But neither do I want to protect them from the knowledge that problems exist. How can we raise children to be honest with us if we give them something less than honesty ourselves? I may not be able to change another person's ways of dealing with life, but even if I can't get the elephant out of my living room right away, I will at least acknowledge that he's sitting there.

DRINKing was angeR and teRROR
zzz

PART TWO

LIVING IN FEAR

A relationship between parental alcoholism and child abuse is indicated in a large proportion of child abuse cases.

▲

Children of alcoholics often never know what to expect from their parents. They can be reared with loving attention or physical abuse. When parents under the influence verbally or physically abuse their children, they often deny any wrongdoing and act as if nothing has happened. The child is left to wonder if anything happened after all. Sometimes the parent withdraws after an abusive episode, having no contact with the child. Other parents try to make amends with smothering affection. Some parents even laugh at their own drunken antics, as if their misbehavior were a harmless joke. Life for these children is confusing and unpredictable. But underneath the chaos that is so common in a household with an alcoholic parent is a dangerous undercurrent of physical and mental abuse that invariably leaves children victimized by alcoholism.

LOUIE ANDERSON

from
Dear Dad: Letters from an Adult

In this excerpt, comedian Louie Anderson works through some of the shame, anger, and sadness of his childhood through a series of letters written to his dead father. In one of the letters he recalls an afternoon he spent with this father, one that ended in a car crash caused by his father's drinking. His dad's irresponsible behavior is only made worse by his refusal to recognize the serious nature of the crash. Anderson's father's behavior is played out tens of thousands of times each year by drinking parents who can't even find the strength to protect their children from the dangerous and thoughtless actions brought on by intoxication.

Anderson grew up with eleven brothers and sisters in the projects of St. Paul, Minnesota. His alcoholic father, a one-time musician with Hoagy Carmichael's band, was abusive, and his mother only enabled his behavior. On many occasions, his mother suggested it was the children's behavior that led their father to drink.

Anderson learned to diffuse the pain through laughter, in an effort to constructively remember his childhood. He has appeared on the *Tonight* show, on HBO and Showtime specials, and in *Coming to America* with Eddie Murphy.

Dear Dad,

It's been a long day. It started with a phone call early this morning. I've never been a morning person. Either were you. It was Mom who called. She wanted to see if her room was ready. Not here, of course. Not in my house. I have fifty-four stairs up to the front door. She's only visited me once. From then on, she's always stayed in hotels.

We're going to Las Vegas together. Not together, actually—we're going to meet there. Did you ever fly with Mom? From the time the plane takes off till the time it lands, she gives you the history of the world from her perspective. It boils down to salt and pepper shakers and oak furniture and whose kids are on drugs.

One time we went to Europe together. It was a thirteen-hour flight. Twenty minutes into it I turned to her and said, "Mom, you've got to shut up. I love you, but I don't care about Woolworth's anymore." After an hour I had strapped on five seat cushions and was looking for an exit.

Dad, it's so funny how, whenever I start talking about

the family, everything turns into a routine. I bet I have one hour of material on you and Mom alone. Being one of eleven children is, for a comedian, like falling into a gold mine. I started developing my routines at the breakfast table, staring at Tommy. "Mom, Louie's looking at me," he'd say in a whiny, baby voice.

I remember doing that to him. God, that used to drive him crazy. My response to Mom was great.

"What? Is it against the law to look at people?"

She'd go back to fixing breakfast, and I'd mumble, "Hey, Tommy, what happened to your hair?"

"What?" he would say.

"Your hair, it looks like a girl's hair."

He would march back upstairs and comb it until it looked different. Then he'd rejoin breakfast. I wouldn't look at him at first, and then, all of a sudden, he would look up and I would be staring at him, smiling.

"Whaddya looking at?" he'd say.

"My new little sister, Thomasina."

He would swear under his breath.

"Oh, my dirty-mouthed little sister," I'd snipe.

That's the kind of stuff that can put someone over the edge. It would never get that far if you were at the table, but you were rarely there. You were either sleeping off a drunk or at your early-morning job.

Tommy and I were always the little ones, numbers ten

and eleven. We were almost like grandchildren. I was so mad when he was born. I was supposed to be the last kid. The baby. Then he came along. I vowed to destroy him. That's what little brothers are for, isn't it?

Ironically, over the years it's worked out that, of everyone in the family, we're the closest to each other. I call him all the time just to ask, "How's my little sister, Thomasina?"

Anyway, Mom wanted me to have a rundown on the whole family before we meet in Vegas. Funny thing is, she only wants to talk about the ones who are doing well. But the more I think about all of us, it's amazing that we're not all in a mental institution. Of course, some of us Andersons have spent some time behind locked doors or bars of one kind. People don't usually admit they have crazy people in their family, but they're coming from somewhere. There isn't just one couple in Minnesota having them all.

I guess the thing that drove me crazy was your drinking, and nobody in the family really wants to talk about that—except me. I want to talk about it. Let's talk about it, Dad. What do you have to say?

Mom said that you always drank, but that it didn't start affecting you until you got a little older. That's how she remembers it, anyway. I remember that you always drank and that it always affected you. It affected me, anyway. You were already fifty years old when I was born, so, compared to other kids, I had an older father, almost a grandfather.

I can remember coming home from school and knowing when I walked in the door whether or not you had been drinking—without even seeing anyone. That's how sensitive I think I became. I could just tell by instinct when you had been drinking. When you drank at night, you'd sit in the room right next to the kitchen, and every time you sipped, the back of your head would tilt back around the corner. We'd see your head bob up and down like a cork floating in a pool.

We would often anticipate how the night would go by how much you would drink. Usually, you'd buy a case of beer and wouldn't go to bed until you drank every last drop. Occasionally, I would work up my nerve and, when you would go into the bathroom, I'd open a couple bottles and pour them out. I guess that was my way of saying, "Please don't drink any more."

We all knew the night was going to get really bad when you downed the last beer and then pulled out a gallon of wine. The stress on us was enormous. Exhausted after one of these evenings, I would fall into bed, only to be woken up a few hours later by a voice loud enough to rattle windows. You'd be calling Mom a whore. Lots of times then, you'd open my door, flick on the light, and yell, "Hey, lard ass, when ya going to lose some weight?"

I don't think you loved me. Maybe you did, but I never felt it. I wonder how the rest of the family felt? No one talks about it, but your drinking did affect us. Roger, Rhea, Jim, Bill, Shanna, they all drank. I did, too, for a while. Like me, they all found a way to quit. But, Dad, your problem became my problem, all our problem.

The really sick part is that somehow I have always blamed myself for your drinking problem. Maybe if he hadn't had so many children, I think. Maybe if I wasn't born at all. Maybe if I had done more to help everyone. Maybe if there hadn't been so much pressure on you to pay so many bills. Maybe then you wouldn't have drunk.

Maybe not.

I don't know. I'd like to know, but I don't know how to find out.

Signed,
An impressionable son

Dear Dad,

A few hours ago I was at the bank, and a nice woman came up to me and said, "Oh, you're the comedian who doesn't use the *F*-word."

"I use it all the time," I said. " 'Family.' It's the dirtiest word I know."

She laughed and said, "No, not that one. The other *F*-word."

"You couldn't mean me," I smiled, "because I use that one all the time, too."

"You do?"

"Sure." I nodded. " 'Father.' It's right up there with 'family.' Almost interchangeable."

She laughed, asked for an autograph, and then left me alone. But it's true, Dad. Words are only dirty depending on your relationship to them. The really bad ones that most people think of were the ones I heard all the time growing up. They came out like an afterthought of your drinking. Put the booze in and the blue language came out until it ceased to have an effect on any of us.

Of course, "family" is a word that was rarely used in the Anderson household. And "father" is a word that had so many different meanings to all of us. To me, "Wait till your father gets home" has always been the single most terrifying sentence anyone could utter. I never knew if you'd be mean or kind, if you'd yell at me or insult me. I only had to hear that and I'd begin thinking about my own favorite *F*-word.

Food.

Not that you're asking, but I think my success in comedy has as much to do with talent as it does with this relentless inner drive I have for wanting to make people love me. In a way, I also want to succeed to compensate for your frustration at having to quit show business. But more than anything, I guess, I really want to be bathed and coddled in the applause of an audience.

It has nothing to do with ego. Things were always chaotic when I was little, and I grew up feeling the uncertainty, shame, and danger of a volatile home life. Because of your drinking, there was a lot of fighting in the house. I never knew if it was my fault or not, but somehow always felt that I played a part in whatever troubled you. As a result, I never felt the security that allows a child to grow up feeling loved.

You fled whatever demons plagued you in cheap alcohol. My escape was food. As you drank and got drunk, I ate and got big. The more frightened I got, the more I ate and the bigger I grew. The more unloved I felt, the more I ate and the bigger I got.

Of course, comedy was my deliverance. I learned to turn the prickly side of life into punchlines. But I haven't been able to turn the punchlines into happiness. I still eat too much, I'm still trying to fill the enormous emotional void inside me by filling myself with food and hoping the warm, soothing comfort of a full belly will last forever. It never does.

Dad, the way I see it, you died without ever confronting your innermost fears, and I'm not going to allow myself to follow the same route. That would be too easy for me. I could sit behind the electric gate of my home and have food delivered every day and never go outside and just eat until I exploded. I could be like you, Dad. But I don't want to be.

I want to change. I want to be happy. And I think the key to understanding my problems is to understand you and your behavior. Your behavior had so much to do with the way I am and the way I don't want to be anymore. I knew you for twenty-seven years and, unfortunately, I really know very little about you as a person. Did you love me? I'd like to know. It's the biggest mystery of my life, and I'm going to try to solve it.

Signed,
Too big to hide

Dear Dad,

It's too bad you never got the chance to see my house. It's way up in the Hollywood Hills, and every room has a panoramic view of the city as it spreads out seemingly forever. Tonight the cool desert air is blowing, and the sky is crystal clear. Nights like these have an almost medicinal effect on the soul.

When I first came to Los Angeles, I drove up into the hills and looked out over the city just as I'm doing now. It was then I decided that I would one day live in the hills.

Five years passed before I could afford to get a place up here, but the thought never left my mind. When you have a view as far as you can see, there don't seem to be any limits. Growing up as I did, I thought of nothing but limits. "Be a good child, Louie," Mom always told me. "Don't cause problems. Don't act up. We don't want your father to start drinking."

What a bunch of crap, making me think that my actions caused you to drink.

Your drinking has always been the riddle of my existence. Why, Dad, why'd you drink?

You know, my earliest memory in life is when I was five years old. I was hiding under the kitchen table with Tommy while you were hitting Mom. You were drunk, naturally. You slapped her across the face and called her a whore. Your voice thundered through our tiny duplex like a violent storm. I remember Jim bolted in the front door and pinned you against the refrigerator.

"Don't ever, ever, do that again!" he yelled right into your droopy face.

The rest of us watched in horror from the other room. I don't know what frightened us more. That you hit Mom. Or that, once you sobered up and realized what had happened, you'd get drunk and angry all over again. Mom had a look on her face that seemed to say, "Oh, what am I going to do now?" As in every crisis, she went to the kitchen sink, turned on the faucet, and washed her hands.

Later, you and Jim sipped coffee at the kitchen table and talked in hushed voices. Mom was in the living room with us, trying to listen in on your conversation as she straightened the doilies on the sofa. She ran her hands over those doilies over and over again, smoothing them as if she were soothing someone's pain. Her pain, your pain, everyone's pain.

I went over to her and put my hand on her arm and began to rub it. I wanted to make her feel better.

"It's OK," she said to me. "Don't worry."

"But why did Daddy hit you?" I asked.

"He was just angry."

"Why?"

"He was upset at himself."

"But why, Mom?"

She didn't ever answer me. Instead, Mom went into the kitchen, started the water running in the kitchen sink, and fixed me something to eat. This seemed to signal an end to the troubles. You got up from the table, parked yourself in front of the TV, and rolled a Bull Durham. Meanwhile, the riddle of my existence continued unexplained.

A few years later, I remember, you and I were out doing errands for Mom. We went by this store and I saw this road racer that cost $4.88. I wanted it badly, like kids get stuck on things. But you said we couldn't afford it. We continued on and then you went into a liquor store and bought a case of beer that cost five dollars. "God," I thought, "that's more important than me? Why was I even born?"

It's always been a mystery to me. We lived at 1122 Hazelwood Avenue, a four-bedroom duplex in the Roosevelt Housing Projects. Mom always boasted that we were one of the first families to move in, but I always wondered what was so great about that. I knew that we were poor. None of the families on TV were like ours. Beaver and Wally Cleaver didn't get their clothes from the welfare store.

I remember the welfare lady's monthly visits to our house. She'd spend about an hour talking to you and Mom, the three of you figuring a budget for the family on this lined paper that had all our names on it. Mom would ask if she wanted something to eat, the signal that it was time to leave. Then you'd walk her to the door and thank her for her help.

"You know, Ora," you'd say to Mom after the door shut, "she's such a helpful woman. We ought to get her a present, a really nice present, like a razor-blade necklace."

When I think about it, I realize that I never questioned that we were poor. We just were and that was it. But there were so many other questions. The Wilsons and their red-headed sons lived in the unit that adjoined ours, and I always wondered why you liked to beat up poor Mr. Wilson.

Most times it started the same way. You'd come home after drinking someplace and stand on the porch, yelling, "Come on out, you chicken-shit bastard!" Mom would be peeking out the window, and I'd have a glass to the wall, trying to hear what the Wilsons were saying about you. "Come on out, Wilson," you'd continue, "so I can kick your ass."

"Mom," I'd ask, "why's Dad want to kill Mr. Wilson?"

"Shuush!" she'd say, leaving another riddle unsolved.

By this time, though, everyone was gathered in the living room, huddled together, laughing out of nervousness. Mom ventured to the doorway and tried to persuade you inside. But you wouldn't have any of it. Mr. Wilson had come out and was standing in his doorway.

"Listen, Louie, calm down," he said.

"Don't tell me to calm down, goddamnit," you'd snarl.

"Please don't talk to him, Mr. Wilson," I'd be thinking. "Shut your door. Go back inside. Don't fuel the fire. If you retreat, he'll return to us, and we know how to handle him. We have it down to a science. Please don't let him beat you up again. I can't face your kids anymore, looking at me like it's my fault, like I'm the one who beat you up."

But it was too late. Lisa would turn from the window and give us the latest report. "Oh, he hit him."

With the first blow I'd have the glass up to the wall. "Someone's crying at the Wilsons'," I'd say. "Lisa, what's going on out there?"

"Jim and the boys are trying to break it up," she'd say.

A few minutes would pass, the door would open, and Jim would escort you inside. There'd be blood on your hands. Not your blood. Mom would rush in with a wet, warm cloth to wash off the blood. She'd take care of her baby, calm him down, and the rest of us would disappear.

"Too bad Mr. Wilson can't fight," I'd tell Tommy.

Secretly, I always wished someone would deck you,

just once, but the one time I saw you splayed out frightened me in a way your abuse never did. It was a weekend afternoon and you and I were the only ones home. I was watching TV and heard a horrible crash. You were drunk and had fallen down the basement stairs. You were lying there, unconscious. I raced downstairs and tried to get you up. But I couldn't. So I put a pillow under your head and sat there until Mom got home.

"Why is Dad like this?" I asked Mom.

"He's drunk," she said matter-of-factly.

"Why?"

"He's been drinking."

"But why?"

But why, Dad? I'd still really like to know the answer. It's something I think about when I'm sitting on my balcony on a clear night, gazing at the view of the city.

Signed,
Extremely curious

Dear Dad,

I just settled into my seat, the last seat in first class, and, lucky me, the one next to it is also empty, so I have the whole aisle to myself. It'll be easy for me to get up and tell the people in coach what a nice buffet we have up here. Even so, I hate flying. The airlines lie to you. When the planes are late, they always blame the weather. When there's a mechanical problem, they never know what's wrong. No way would you let them pull that on you, Dad.

I wish you were with me right now so you could give the plane the once-over. You know, kick the tires, check the engines, check the battery cables, and rough up the pilot. We're sitting on the runway now, delayed, the flight attendant just announced, because of the air traffic. I can just imagine what your response would've been.

"Christ," you would've said, "these pilots drive like your mother. If I took the wheel, this bucket would be up."

"But, Dad," my response would've been, "you don't know how to fly."

"Doesn't matter. I was in the war. I can do anything."

The one good thing about this delay is that the stewardess is breaking out the peanuts early—at least in first class. Peanuts are important on a flight. You don't want to go down on an empty stomach. If the stewardess forgets to serve me, I always clear my throat, hoping to quietly catch her attention and point out the error. If she still fails to notice, I usually raise my hand and politely ask, "Excuse me, but am I in the nonpeanut section?"

Meanwhile, wish me a merry Christmas. I'm on my way from sunny Los Angeles to the deep freeze of Minneapolis, our homeland, to personally oversee and orchestrate my Christmas present to me. This is our first family reunion since the dark day of your funeral in 1979. I've given plane tickets to everyone who needed them, except for Billy, who unpredictably wanders in and out of each of our lives. The only catch was, everyone had to agree to my ulterior motive: to talk about you in front of my video camera.

Strangely, I don't know what to expect from the gathering. I never remember Christmas being much fun for our family. I mean, God, it was never the right tree. There was no money for presents. Worst of all, holidays gave you an excuse to drink as much as you wanted.

We won't have to worry about anyone drinking this year. Everyone who drank—four in all—has quit. But your disease afflicted our family in other ways that I now see clearly by looking at how the lives of my brothers and sisters have developed. Kent has spent some time in prison. Rhea married an abusive husband. Roger was horrible to his wife and kids until he gave up liquor. Shanna, who had an abusive, alcoholic husband, didn't turn her life around till she went through a Twelve Step program. Who knows what happened to Billy? And Jim,

Mary, Lisa, Sheila, and Tommy have all struggled, too.

As for me, I can't believe this whole thing is coming off according to plan.

Got to break for dinner and make an announcement to the rest of the plane. I'll let you know what happens.

Signed,
We're getting ready to eat

Dear Dad,

You remember that time we went into the woods, and not by choice? I should've bolted upright and told you a big "Fuck you!" I was only twelve years old. Mom didn't want you going out. She knew you would drink as soon as you were free from her watchful eyes. To get around her, though, you took me and Tommy along. Used us, didn't you? Said, "It's OK, Ora, I've got some errands to do, and I'll take the boys with me."

I didn't want to go on this particular outing. Just as I could tell if you'd been drinking before I walked in the door from school, I could sense the real reason you wanted us to tag along, and it wasn't because you wanted a father-son outing. First you gassed up the car at Joe's.

Joe's, I remember, always had bulk oil for ten cents a quart. That was so appealing—anything for a dime. It sounded like such a good deal. I could never figure out how he made any money on a quart of oil, but I bet he made plenty on the gas.

After filling up, everything seemed great, and I was thinking, "Well, maybe we can have fun."

"Hey," you said, "you guys want to get some pop?"

"Where?" I asked.

"Next door."

There was a bar next to Joe's.

"It's starting to snow," I said. "Shouldn't we do our errands and get back home?"

"Ah, come on," you urged. "It's only for a minute."

"But, Dad. . . ?" I whined.

"You fucking baby, come on."

What choice did I have? What twelve-year-old boy wants to be called a fucking baby by his father? Though I was upset, the three of us went inside and sat atop the high stools along the bar. I ordered a Pepsi and Tommy had an Orange Crush, and there we sat, nursing our sodas for three long, tedious, horrible hours. Tommy and I watched in silence as you tossed back beer after beer, getting drunker and drunker and ruder and ruder, hating every second of this nightmarish drinking bout.

It was dark when the bartender finally kicked us out.

Actually, he tossed you out and we had to follow.

Meanwhile, the weather had gotten more severe. By the time we got outside, it was snowing heavily, one of those still, stormy nights that are beautiful and frightening at the same time. The white so pure, the sky so gray and ominous. You were really drunk, totally pissed and bleary-eyed. I had a weird experience then, a realization where I was suddenly able to view everything that was happening from afar. It was the first time I can remember seeming to be outside of my body. I saw these three pathetic figures standing alone out in front of the bar in the snow, one of them obliterated, the other two terribly frightened. The scene seemed a foreshadowing of a disaster.

The next moment we were in the car. We were the only ones on the road, our Bonneville making the first tracks in the virgin snow. You drove very slow. We traveled down Avenue B, then made a left onto Ames Avenue, cruising by my grade school. I was thinking, "Maybe you could stop and let me out. I could go inside and wait there until tomorrow morning." I've always liked the idea of being inside a school all alone, no one there to pick on me.

However, we continued driving down the winding road, our speed holding steady, me steering from the side, and you hacking out that disgusting smoker's cough, sounding as if broken bottles were being raked inside your throat, and laughing at the situation as if it was some kind of joke that we were in such a frightening circumstance. Two turns before we reached home, you started to nod out.

"Let me drive, Dad," I said.

"Shut up, Louie," you snapped.

"But you're falling asleep."

"I can drive," you insisted.

What the hell were you thinking? We made the turn on Jessimere okay, but there was just one more turn before we were home. Suddenly, though, the car stopped. It wasn't the engine. No, you were out cold. What an ugly picture. The three of us huddled in the front seat—Tommy on the door, me in the middle, and you in the driver's seat, letting out loud, raspy snores. Outside, the snow was falling without letup.

Home wasn't that far, but I was too frightened to get out and run for help. Why? I wanted to protect you, Dad. One of the neighbors might've found out that you were a drunk, that you could've cared less about your kids, that you were willing to risk our lives so you could get some booze. See, none of us knew who was aware of your problem; we were shamed by it.

Somehow, though, I mustered up my courage—a moment of sheer desperation, I'm sure—woke you up, and told you in the gentlest of ways to put the car in gear and step on the brake so I could slowly guide the car home. But because you were so drunk, you stepped on the gas instead. The car took off, heading at a swift pace for the place we all referred to as "the woods."

The landscape was a stark, seamless blanket of white, and everything went flying by so fast. Your heavy foot slipped, and the car was floored. We went careening along the roadside, churning up snow and mud, the Bonneville doors being pounded by tree after tree. It sounded as if we were being shot at. However, despite the speed, I noticed the smallest of details whizzing by. I saw the numbers outside apartments, people eating dinner, my dead grandmother sitting in a rocking chair with perfect clarity. It's what I imagine dying is like. You are on your way out, but not before you see certain things.

In a matter of seconds we flew right over the hill, leaping above the embankment, airborne. I expected a crash, a fiery crash, and then certain death. Instead, we landed in the deep snowdrift with an unexpected *poof.* It was silent. The snow came up like powder and covered the car. I checked to see if you were all right, Dad. There were no injuries. Tommy was unhurt, too. I told him to stay with you in the car while I got out and hiked to our house for help. I could see it in the distance. The light was on, and I could make out the shadows of people in the living room.

Heading toward home, I reached the bottom of the big, icy hill where we always slid on cardboard boxes or our metal discs. I started to climb, but the first two times I came sliding back down, not quite able to reach the top. On my third attempt, I slid down again. But that time it was kind of fun, and for a moment I forgot all about you and Tommy being stuck in the car. When I finally reached the top, a neighbor pulled up in his car, rolled down the window, and asked if I needed any help.

"Nope," I said. "Everything is great. I'm just going home."

Fortunately, when I arrived at home, some of my older brothers were there. I told them what happened, and they went off and rescued you and Tommy from becoming ice cubes in the deep freeze. Not surprisingly, you hardly woke up as they carried you to bed, and you slept until late the next day. You never apologized, either. You handled it by making fun of the incident, laughing at what could've been my early death. Well, Dad, screw you!

Signed,
A backseat driver

Dear Dad,

Why don't I know you better?

I figure that you spent several hours a day for 40 years drinking. Multiply that by 365 days, then divide by 60 minutes, and then divide again by 24 hours. That's more than 1,000 days you spent with alcohol.

In other words, that's more than three years you spent with alcohol instead of your family.

I was alive for twenty-seven of those years, and I missed you.

Signed,
Counting the days

BARBARA DAVIS "B. D." HYMAN

from
My Mother's Keeper

Alcoholism is a disease without conscience or prejudice. It thrives in every family—from the very poor to the very rich, from average ones to the most famous ones, and in educated households as well as the most ignorant ones. To an outsider Barbara Davis Hyman appeared to be one lucky girl, with wealth, clothes, toys, travel, security, and loving parents. In reality her household was chaotic. Her stepfather was violent and unpredictable. Her mother was the mega–Hollywood star Bette Davis, who, emotionally dependent, contributed to Hyman's tumultuous upbringing.

In this excerpt Hyman describes life with her mother's fourth husband, an abusive alcoholic.

When I was eight, we returned to California for Mother to make *The Virgin Queen*, and Gary stayed behind in Maine. Things had again been going badly in their marriage, and the fact that Gary hadn't seen fit to go to work in a long time and money was in short supply didn't help matters. My memories of those next few months are a blur of friends' houses lived in until the friends returned and of cheap rentals, all for the purpose of cutting down on expenses. The best thing was that we had got away from Gary.

While we were in our duplex on East River Drive in New York, our household had been comparatively peaceful. Aside, that is, from the occasional faint sounds of strife that filtered down from Mother and Gary's second-floor suite. It was most likely that things were as bad as ever without my knowing it. It wasn't until the hectic months of searching for and then settling into Witch-Way had given over to the regular routine of everyday life that I was again assaulted by the inescapable sounds of violence. At first Mother seemed to be able to spare the rest of us the worst of it by containing the raging battles behind the closed doors of their suite, but as the struggles became fiercer and the anger more intense, it must have been that only her own survival was on her mind.

My room at Witch-Way was at the top of the staircase at one end of the hallway, while the master suite was a long way away at the other end. As the fights got louder and louder and their door was left open, it became impossible for me to pretend that nothing was happening, impossible to ignore it by hiding my head under my pillow. The noises penetrated, and I couldn't stop myself from listening, from straining to understand what was happening. As long as I could hear Mother shouting back at Gary, I knew she was all right. But when I couldn't hear her anymore, I would open my door and listen for her. When there was only the sound of her weeping and pleading among Gary's threats and name-calling, my fear for Mother would overcome my terror of Gary, and I would find myself irresistibly drawn down the hall to protect my mother. Once in their presence, I wouldn't be able to talk. Mother would look at me, usually from the floor at Gary's feet, and scream, "Get out! Go away!" as she rocked and moaned. Looking back, I'm sure that she only wanted to protect me from Gary, but at the time, it seemed as though she were rejecting my help and it hurt. Gary would glare at me, face contorted into a vicious mask, and shout, "Get away from me and mind your own business, you little slut, or I'll give you the same as your mother! Would you like that . . . huh?" Then he would lurch a step or two in my direction while Mother shouted, "Gary, no! Don't! God, please no! B.D., run! Get out! Now!" I would scream, "Don't hurt Mommy anymore! Don't hit her again!" and Gary would slap me across the face or knock me down and Mother would scream louder that I was making it worse.

Whatever Gary's treatment of Mother and me, he was always careful to shield Michael, whom he adored, from the worst of it. Before beginning one of his rampages, Gary invariably took my brother to his room and locked him in. Then, when the battles were over, Gary would often go to Michael and tell him that he didn't think he would be able to put up with Mommy much longer, that the two of them might have to run away soon. Gary was also likely to burst into tears and fall asleep curled up on Michael's bed with his arms around his little son.

One night I went to bed while a party was going on. It was very noisy, and with guests milling on the lawn beneath my windows, it was impossible for me to fall asleep. As I lay there listening to the conversations below, a heated argument broke out between Gary and another man. The man was accusing Gary of having an affair with his wife, and I recalled the few times I had walked into the living room early in the morning only to freeze in my tracks and quietly back out upon seeing Gary sprawled on the couch with his best friend's wife. I wondered if that was the wife now in question and found it rather pleasing to listen to this man raging at Gary. There was lots of arguing and then the sounds of doors slamming and people leaving. All was quiet for a while, and then I heard Mother shouting at Gary in the entry hall at the bottom of the stairs. "You make me sick! You think you're such a hotshot with all the broads? *Ha!* You haven't laid *me* in years. The only time you touch me is when you beat me up. *Bastard!* That's all you're good at." Then came Gary's evil laugh and sneering tones. "What are you bitching about? Getting slapped around is the only thing you enjoy, you stupid cunt! If it doesn't do anything for you, why do you beg for it all the time?"

"Oh, my God! That's what you always say, and you know it isn't true. You know that violence terrifies me. All I want is to be loved like a woman."

"*Bullshit!* You're no woman . . . you're a frigging ice queen. Without an audience you're not worth a shit! Maybe if I knocked you on your frigid ass on the stage of the London Palladium and then jumped you, you'd perform. Outside of that, a knothole in a tree is more exciting than you."

"*Jesus!* You really are something! I suppose all the other men in my life didn't know what they were talking about? One of them even—"

"*Jesus Christ!* Are you going to hand me that crap about Howard Hughes screwing you on a bed of gardenias again? He fucked every two-bit twat in Hollywood, and you're proud of holding out for ten bucks' worth of gardenias! Poor dumb son of a bitch wasted a lot of flowers. The only people who can be around you for long without wanting to kill you are faggots, so don't waste your time telling me about all the men—"

"So my other three husbands were fags, were they? Well let me tell *you* something . . . at least *they* were men! They—"

"*They* nothing! They all kicked the shit out of you. You've told everybody who would listen to you about it. The first was a nothing, the second was a drunk who never left his mommy's titty, and the third ran away with your slut daughter's nurse. The only thing I'll say for them is that they got airplanes out of you. You didn't have anything left when I came along."

Mother screamed, "Stop it! Stop it! I can't take any more," and I heard their feet pounding up the stairs. When she reached the top, Mother shrieked, "Get away from me! Go to your whore! I don't want you." A stream of curses and threats filled the night, and I realized that

I had moved from my bed to the door, just a few feet from where they were standing. Mother suddenly whispered a plea that he not " . . . frighten the children." But Gary shouted, apparently directly at my door, "Maybe the little slut should come out and see what you get for starting a fight."

"Gary, get out of my house!" Mother yelled, panic in her voice. "Leave this instant! Leave B.D. out of this for God's sake!" I ran and jumped back into bed, but too late. The door flew open and Gary roared, "You want to listen? You might as well have a clear view as well!" He laughed at me, and Mother threw herself at him like a crazed cat. Gary turned and knocked her to the floor. She tried to get up, and he knocked her down again. She tried to run back down the stairs, I think in an attempt to steer Gary away from me, but he caught her at the top of the stairs. I could see her flailing at him, trying to get loose. He had her by the neck, and, as she got down a couple of steps, he moved to the other side of the railing and jerked her along until her feet could no longer touch ground and she dangled by her neck while he bellowed about teaching her a real lesson. Mother was making gurgling, choking noises, and I couldn't stand it anymore. I flung myself at Gary's back, pummeling him with my fists, trying to make him let go of her. I screamed hysterically, "You're killing her, you're killing her!" He kicked me away a couple of times. Mother was just hanging there, thrashing wildly and choking. I couldn't just give up. This time he was going to kill her. Oh, how I wished somebody would hear and come to help, but there wasn't a soul stirring anywhere despite all the noise. Suddenly Gary let go of Mother and she fell halfway down the stairs, to the landing directly below her. I wanted to run to help her but Gary spun around, hit me and flattened me against the wall. I must have passed out because I don't remember anything more until I woke up on my bed.

There were voices coming from the front hall, and to my overwhelming relief I heard Mother's. Then I heard Gary's laughter and amiable tones, then strange male voices. I got up and, feeling sore all over, made my way to the top of the stairs, where I crouched to hear what was going on. Mother was pacing wildly and flapping her arms. Gary was sitting on the hall bench with his legs crossed, drink in hand, swirling the ice cubes casually around in his glass and smiling benignly at two uniformed policemen. Mother was shrieking half incoherently at the policemen, showing them her neck and accusing Gary of trying to strangle her. One of the policemen tried to explain, evidently not for the first time, that unless she were willing to press charges, which would necessitate them taking Gary off to jail, there was nothing else they could do. Mother said that she didn't want it in the newspapers but that they should do something informally. The policeman said his hands were tied and turned his attention to Gary when Mother became increasingly hysterical. Gary explained that it had been a simple domestic argument, winked knowingly and said that he was sure they knew how that was. He said that it was really nothing for them to concern themselves with and that his wife was prone to overreaction and hysteria, as he was sure they could see for themselves. Then he offered them a drink. I wanted to run downstairs, but then Gary would clobber me again after the policemen left. I stayed where I was, and when it was all over, I scurried back to my room. My toy poodle, Tinker Bell, was curled up on my bed. I snuggled close to her, glad of something warm and friendly to love and by whom to be loved. I could understand *her*.

Gary continued to come and go at random intervals and was drunk far more often than he was sober. I didn't make a conscious decision about my plight, but it slowly dawned on me that if Mother had minded Gary's attacks and all the violence, she would have done something about it. I was sick not only of being slapped around by Gary, but even more of the constant fear and uncertainty his mere presence engendered in me. I began to stay out of their fights as much as I could, no matter how much it seemed as though he were about to kill Mother. Sometimes he came straight at me without first attacking Mother, and I gradually developed the ability to detect a change in the tone of his voice. When that change came and I was quick enough, I got out of the house before the fighting began. I had several hiding places, two of which he never found, one behind some bushes on the hillside overlooking the pool, the other behind the vine-covered chain-link fence that surrounded the tennis court. He rarely failed to search for me, but, more often than not, I evaded him. It entailed my sleeping out of doors in my secret places and creeping to my bed at dawn, but it was worth it. By that time, Gary had forgotten.

In June we packed up again and went to Maine for the summer. Sally came too and continued to be my best friend. I got up every morning at dawn and rode endlessly. I was constantly in trouble for missing meals. By this time I was very good at horse and stable management, and the housekeeper was heard to bewail the fact that "Miss B.D. keeps her stable far better than she keeps her room." It took a while, but when Mother discovered how early I was taking to horse, she promptly banned it, announcing that she did not approve of a young girl being up and out at dawn. Eight o'clock and later, it seemed, met with her approval, but not earlier. Arguing the matter brought me nothing but "It isn't the proper thing for my daughter to do. *Brother!* Just get off my back about it."

Mother always had tacit lists of things of which she did and did not "approve." Her highest compliment, in her view, was to tell me that she approved of me. I never nailed down exactly what she meant by this, but she always glowed when saying it. She did not approve of asking what was for dinner, talking baby talk to babies (it warped their future speech patterns), artificial flowers, improperly dressed children (properly being the way she dressed *her* children), or houseguests doing anything for themselves without permission or assistance. The things she approved of varied and were never known in advance. She had lists of things she approved of for herself, but different ones for everyone else. She neither realized nor cared that the lists were different and inconsistent, but whether or not she approved of things loomed very large in her legend. She often spoke of her father's disapproval of her and felt the need either to approve or disapprove of everything herself.

My practice of hiding whenever I detected the telltale edge to Gary's voice had become second nature to me.

One night, while I was sleeping in the apple orchard, I was awakened by the sound of a horse's high-pitched screaming, a sound they only make when they are terrified. Thinking that a fire must somehow have broken out in the stable, I sprinted the hundred yards from the orchard and flung myself through the door. The lights were on, and Gary was in Sally's stall with a length of barbed wire in his hand. The mare was plunging hysterically around the stall, banging her knees into the walls and screaming in terror. Gary was holding the wire in a loop above his head and making lunging moves at Sally, quite obviously bent on getting the loop over her head and around her neck. His back was to the stall door. I leaped across the intervening twelve feet, threw the bolt, and flung open the door. Sally plunged through the opening, knocking Gary backward into the wall as she did so, and took off at a mad gallop with me hard on her heels. I went back into hiding, knowing that Sally wouldn't go far, and waited to see what Gary would do next. It wasn't long before he stumbled out of the stable and went to the house. I waited five more minutes, to be on the safe side, then found Sally and led her back to the stable. Her neck, shoulders and face were badly lacerated, her knees were banged up and she was lame. I spent the rest of the night treating her wounds and poulticing her knees. In the morning Gary drove off and I went in search of Mother. I told her what had happened and insisted that she come to see Sally. She resisted strenuously, arguing that she didn't " . . . have to walk all the way to the stable just to see a couple of scratches on a horse," but I eventually prevailed and got her down there. She glanced at Sally and said, "Gary's an idiot. He was roaring drunk and probably decided to go for a ride in the middle of the night."

"If that were the case, Mother," I demanded angrily, "why was he in her stall slashing at her with barbed wire?"

"He probably mistook it for a lead rope," she replied and walked away.

Summer came to an end. Mother and Gary got ready for their tour of the country with *The World of Carl Sandburg*, a dramatic reading of Sandburg's works that was to receive great acclaim. Mother enrolled Michael and me at Chadwick School in southern California, in second and seventh grades, respectively. This was Michael's first time at boarding school, and I was all set to play mother; however, within a couple of weeks he, as well as I, had a whole set of buddies, and the last thing he wanted was a big sister breathing down his neck. At

Chadwick, thank heavens, we weren't outcasts. There were all sorts of film children there, including Liza Minnelli, and we were just two more. Sally had again crossed the country, since the school provided boarding facilities for students who had their own horses. The condition of boarding was that the students care for their own stock. I arose at five each day, walked the half mile to the stables, fed, watered, and mucked out, then hotfooted it back to the dorm to shower, change, and get to breakfast by seven-thirty. I rode most days after classes and taught Sally and myself to jump. There was plenty of room to ride on campus, and the Chadwicks were very lenient, provided that we used good judgment.

During Christmas vacation Mother and Gary rented the house at Laguna Beach where I was born. Margot was flown in from her school in New York State, and Mother, who was always very emotional about Christmas, believed that despite the almost total deterioration of her relationship with Gary, we would have one big happy reunion. All I can recall of that Christmas is we children tiptoeing around, trying not to be held responsible for starting the next shouting match; that and the fact that I pleaded with Mother to leave Gary. Whenever we were all in the same place at the same time, it was the same story: fights, beatings, curses, and screaming. If Gary was there, the rest was sure to follow.

At Easter vacation Michael and I were flown up to San Francisco to join Mother and Gary, who were there doing the final performances of the northern leg of the Sandburg tour. When we arrived, we found a situation that so frightened us that we locked ourselves in our rooms for most of the time. The shouting and screaming, not to mention the crashings and bangings, were enough to frighten anyone, let alone the seven- and eleven-year-old children of the antagonists.

Tennessee Williams was in San Francisco for a meeting with Mother concerning the possibility of her doing *The Night of the Iguana* on Broadway. His go-between was a lady by the name of Viola Rubber. Viola was aware of the situation between Gary and Mother, as must have been everyone else in the hotel, and she was nice enough to take Michael and me on outings to Fisherman's Wharf and Top of the Mark and on as many cable-car rides as we wanted. Just before we were to go back to school, Mother told us that she had finally come to terms with the fact that she had to divorce Gary. I was immensely relieved, but Michael took it very badly.

June arrived, and another school year came to a close. Michael, Sally, and I returned to Maine for what was to be our last summer there. After Mother's announcement in San Francisco, and knowing that Gary had been replaced in the southern leg of the Sandburg tour by Barry

Sullivan, the last person I expected to see when I got to Maine was Gary, but there he was, and nothing had changed. Gary would argue that there was no real reason for them to get divorced, and Mother would sometimes stand her ground and sometimes give in, but, whatever her posture of the moment, either immediately or within a few hours they were once more shouting and throwing things. Gary would then leave, only to reappear unannounced and do it all again.

Mother was utterly miserable but was determined to put a good face on things. It was obvious to everyone who knew us that divorce was inevitable, but she kept postponing the actuality. Her marriage to Gary was to have been the marriage to end all marriages, and she simply could not bring herself to accept another failure.

Many friends came and went that summer, including the Batchelder family, whom Mother had known for most of her life. She and Ellen Batchelder had been friends since their teens. Their daughter, Gay, was about my age and an avid horsewoman to boot. We hit it off immediately and formed what was to be a lifelong friendship. Mother, entirely of her own volition, had the idea that it would be nice if Gay and I could ride together and rented an extra horse for the duration of the Batchelders' stay. It made that last summer in Maine even more special for me.

Giving up her marriage to Gary was the most heartbreaking thing Mother ever had to do. It wasn't that there was any tenderness, let alone love, left between them. It was that she had to forsake her self-image of successful wife and mother, roles she had always held to be more important than any others. She was convinced that Gary was her last chance to maintain that image, and rather than accept the shattering of the image, she had hidden for a very long time behind an emotional smoke screen.

Upon her divorce, Mother sold Butternut and Witch-Way. We were sad about this phase of our lives coming to an end. Despite Gary, we had loved our childhood in Maine, and Mother, to her credit, had accomplished her purpose of giving us some basis in reality with a New England rural upbringing. She was convinced, with good reason, that growing up solely in Hollywood would make it impossible for us to have our feet on the ground in later life. The glitter and glamour of Hollywood were all right as a place but not as a philosophy.

The successful wife half of her image was destroyed, and Mother determined never to marry again. There was "no man worth a shit as a husband on the face of the earth. They all let you down. . . . It's just a question of time." She focused all of her hopes for emotional fulfillment on me, proclaiming that I was the most talented, brilliant, beautiful being on earth. I came to pity anyone who failed to rave about me in her presence. According to her, there was nothing and no one good enough for B.D. B.D. was all that remained of her dream, and if nothing else in her life were certain, at least she could rely on that. B.D. was to be the fantasy daughter of the world's greatest mother, and the presents lavished on her would know no bounds. "B.D. is the only thing I have ever really loved."

The fear and the hurt of the last five years were finally over. I had survived. Because Mother had been pulled too many ways at once and had not protected me, I had learned to protect myself. I never doubted that she loved me, and I never had any reason to contemplate my own feelings. She was my mother, and I loved her. She had always been generous with me, and particularly so after Gary had hurt me. Now she loved me more than anything else, and whatever I wanted was mine. I slipped into the new role without a thought. It seemed perfectly natural to equate gifts with love. Whenever I gave Mother a card or a present of any sort, I received an "Oh, thank you, B.D., I'm so happy that you love me so much."

It wasn't that Mother had no love for Michael. She did love him, but it wasn't clear whether she loved him for himself or just as the symbolic son. I had always been

Mother's daughter, and when Gary was angry with her, he also vented his fury on me. Michael, on the other hand, was the apple of Gary's eye, and although Mother got custody of both of us, Michael remained loyal to Gary. Mother, despite protestations to the contrary, deeply resented my brother's inability to accept her as his one and only parent. Whenever Michael returned from visiting Gary, Mother subjected him to merciless cross-questioning. What had Gary said about Mother? What had Michael said about Mother? Whom did Michael love better? How could he love Gary at all when she was the only one who loved *him*? And on and on and on. Michael would sneak into my room at night to pour out his woes and have a good cry. We were probably closer as brother and sister during the next few years than at any other time in our lives.

BETSY PETERSON

from
Dancing with Daddy

When Betsy Petersen first wrote a candid book about her childhood, few family friends wanted to know about her father's dark side. A warm, witty physician with many friends, her father and her mother loved a party—and they had plenty. Her father, a heavy drinker, sexually abused both Petersen and her sister. Her mother, who had drinking problems as well, never cared enough to notice.

In Petersen's upper-middle-class family, entertaining for the evening usually involved drinking excessive amounts of alcohol and ending the evening with slurred speech and loss of memory. In this excerpt she recalls her rage and feelings of powerlessness when faced with her parents' alcoholism.

Drunks

After we moved to the suburbs when I was four, friends of my parents would come down from the city on Saturdays, arriving in time for a late lunch. We would sit on the banquettes at the round kitchen table, eating pickles and nuts and smelly cheese and drinking beer. "Can I have a sip of beer?" I'd ask my father, and he'd say, "Get your little glass." My glass was a small cylinder—cheese spread had come in it—with a blue flower outlined on the side, and my father would pour an ounce of beer into it for me to drink. I can still taste the yeasty bubbles and see the clear amber topped with foam.

My father was fat, and he would stick his stomach out and mock himself. "Pretty soon I'll be so fat you won't be able to sit on my lap," he'd say, and I'd mark the air with my hand where his stomach, sometime in the future, would stick out so far it would make a shelf for me to sit on. "Your daddy's a dirty old man," he'd say, and the friends would laugh.

Sometimes the friends brought children with them, but usually I was the only child at the party. I sat with the grown-ups at the table, listening to the talk, laughing when they laughed, as the afternoon merged into evening and preparations for dinner began.

My parents had a friend I was taught to call Uncle, who often joined the party. Once at the table he tried to kiss me, looking sad like an old dog. I smiled at him so he wouldn't get mad, and turned my head away, and the grown-ups laughed. My father told me later he was an alcoholic, and something called a "remittance man"—his relatives paid him to stay away.

They had another friend, also an alcoholic, a woman my mother always identified as someone from the days "when I was young and poor and lived on Telegraph Hill." One Saturday this woman and "Uncle" went down to the basement—we called it the rumpus room—and went to bed together. I didn't know about it at the time, but in later years I heard my father tell the story often. For him the best part was when he told how the sound rose straight up the heating duct to my sister's bedroom on the floor above. It was meant to be a funny story. My father laughed when he told it, and their friends laughed, and I laughed.

My mother changed when she drank, first her voice and then her face. Right away I could hear her tongue stumbling over consonants, as if she couldn't fit them all into her mouth. And she laughed a lot. When she was sober, her laugh was false: two notes, one in midrange and one above, a Tinker Bell laugh, cute and phony as a glass ring from a gum machine.

But her drinking laugh sounded real. By midafternoon on those Saturdays her laugh, her voice, her face had become hectic, suffused with energy. She looked happy, alive, like her real self, the self she had chosen and wanted to be.

It was years before I realized that my father was getting drunk at those parties, too. He just got quieter and quieter, and late in the evening he'd sit down on the floor with his back against the wall and go to sleep. "Daddy is being a mystic," my sister would say, quoting an empty-headed woman speaking to a drunk in a Peter Arno cartoon. I knew the cartoon, and I knew the man in the cartoon was drunk, but I didn't know my father was drunk. I thought he was sleepy because he worked so hard.

In the daytime, on weekdays, my mother was crabby and distracted. She would snap at me if I annoyed her, sometimes for no reason that I could see, although I believed it was my fault. Yet I often heard her say that I had been a good baby, was a good child; unlike my sister, I never caused any trouble. I took long naps; I went willingly to school; I kept quiet and asked no questions.

I was barely visible to her when she was sober. When she began to drink, I disappeared, becoming like a ghost in a story who tries to communicate with the living but cannot make itself heard. Only once in a while, when she was drinking, would she seem to see me for a moment. She would peer at me, blinking owlishly, and then draw back and laugh, responding to my distress as if it were disapproval, and mocking it. I saw myself through her eyes as the straitlaced, dull bourgeoise, a foil for her glamour and vitality.

Very occasionally on a weekend there was no party at home, and no invitation to go out. When there was no company, only me to hear them, my parents drank and quarreled. One evening when I was eleven or so, I heard them starting up and resolved to stop them. I dressed up in funny clothes and painted my face, interrupting them over and over so they could applaud each new variation of my costume. In the pictures of me my father took that night, I look pretty, flushed with energy; I felt desperate panic.

My father was famous for the strong drinks he mixed for his guests, and once I was there when he put liquor in a drink he mixed for a woman who had reminded him several times that alcohol made her sick. It was his habit at parties—part of his philosophy of life—to mix the first few drinks extra strong, because that helped the party "take off."

When I was in college, I asked him for some Dexedrine to help me study. That was the kind of relationship we had in the story we told ourselves: open, adult, up front about everything. He opened the cabinet in his bathroom and took out a quart bottle full of green tablets. "I got these for Joe," he told me. Joe was a close friend; my father was carrying on a flirtation with his wife. "Joe is an alcoholic," he told me, his voice full of self-importance, the family doctor who can be trusted to tell you the truth. "Sometimes Dexedrine is helpful for that." He doled out some green tablets. "I know you'll be careful with these," he said.

He had a story about Dexedrine. When it first became available, it was manufactured as a syrup, and my father got a bottle of it and put some in the punch at a party. "That party really took off!" he said, with that chortle he had when he'd played a good joke on somebody.

One evening when I was five or six my parents took me with them to spend the evening with some friends. I suppose they couldn't find a baby-sitter, and my sister, who dated every weekend, rarely stayed with me. The friends' children, younger than I, had gone to sleep in their own beds, but I lingered on with the grown-ups, as was my habit at my parents' parties. The husband was in the kitchen with my mother—I could hear them talking in loud voices and laughing. The wife sat on my father's lap in a big easy chair. She lay across the arms of the chair, and he held her loosely, one hand on her thigh. She wore a thin black dress. She had a cloud of wavy black hair and deep, dark eyes, and an ample body. My father looked at her with a foolish smile, his eyes unfocused like the "mystic" in the Peter Arno cartoon, and I sat across the room from them and cried. "Don't you want to go upstairs and lie down?" asked the husband, hearing my sobs. But I wouldn't go. Maybe I was afraid of what my father and the wife might do if I left them alone. I sat on the sofa and cried until my parents took me home.

I saw my father look at my mother that way once, when I was eleven or twelve. They had some grapes they were going to make into wine, and my mother was going to squeeze the juice out of them with her feet. She wore a T-shirt of my father's tied between her legs, and a bandana around her head, as she stepped into the ten-gallon crock. Her voice was high-pitched and slurred, and my father's face looked blurred as he smiled at her with soft, loose lips. It should have been something private for the two of them, but they wanted me to be their witness. I sat on the hard basement steps and played my flute, because they wanted me to. I pretended to have fun, because they wanted me to; but I was very, very tired.

My parents drank beer in the afternoons, cocktails before dinner, and wine with dinner and afterward. They drank jug wine that came in wicker-covered bottles, and poured it into little dark blue glasses they'd bought on Olvera Street in Los Angeles soon after they were married. After dinner they would pile the dirty dishes haphazardly on the kitchen counter and move to the living room, where they would drink glass after glass after glass of wine. If there were guests, there was conversation, which I was taught to consider brilliant and sophisticated. My mother would be in constant motion. Years later my father wrote, "To me she was a completely new species, sometimes gay, sometimes deeply serious; frivolous, fun-loving; sometimes giving with abandon, sometimes demanding imperiously; flitting from one mood to another with such dazzling speed that she blended them all." I remember her party self, her triangular smile, the upper corners drawn up toward the eyes, and the way one eye seemed lower than the other, not in the same latitude. The face of a stranger, not my mother. Her real face.

After everyone else had gone home, one other couple would remain. Usually there was a couple of the moment, somebody my parents were spending most of their free time with. These tandem romances usually lasted a year or two before my parents took up with someone new. My mother and the other man would laugh raucously while my father murmured softly in the woman's ear. My mother would reach out for the bottle of wine and very deliberately pour some into her glass, and then she would set it down very carefully; but in spite of her care it would clunk as it came down to meet the table a little sooner than she expected.

By this time her face would have gone soft, like butter in midsummer. She would peer at her companion in the candlelight, her eyes slitted, her lips soft and moist, pausing before she made another point in the deep conversation they were having. Sometimes she would verbally advance on her foe, trying to corner him. Sometimes she would roll her eyes and purse her lips and look deeply sad, as if to suggest that though she had known grief in her time, she was brave and gallant; nobody knew the trouble she'd seen.

I never knew how these conversations ended, because at some point my mother would ask, offhandedly, if I wanted to go to bed now. In case it was what they wanted, in case it made a difference what I did, I went.

One night when I was in high school I came home and saw my mother dancing around and around on the cork tile floor, swooping and laughing, while my father and their guest, a man I didn't know, egged her on. It was the worst—to me the worst—I'd ever seen her. I hated it, hated her. I pressed my lips together in a thin, disapproving line and spoke of other things in short, clipped sentences, the way we did in our family when we were angry. The next morning my father drove me to school, and in the car I said, my heart pounding, "Mother was really drunk last night." I had never in my life said aloud that either of them got drunk.

"She was fine until you came home," my father said. "She was happy, she was having a good time, and then you came home and made her feel bad."

"I'm afraid she's an alcoholic," I said.

"She's not an alcoholic," he said, his voice irritated, as if he were swatting a fly. He might have been saying: Get away from me. I have enough to take care of, earning enough money to buy your clothes; it isn't fair that I should have to be bothered with this, too.

Loud silence lasted until we arrived at school. I fumbled with the door handle. "Open the door, asshole!" he snarled—the only time he ever called me anything worse than "knothead."

"Don't you call me names!" I shouted. "Don't you ever call me names!" I got out and slammed the door. That night he apologized for calling me "asshole," the only time he ever told me he was sorry for anything. He didn't mention my fears about my mother, then or ever.

I didn't talk about drinking again to either of my parents until thirty years later, after my father died. Over lunch in a restaurant my mother said, "You're awfully quiet."

"I want to ask you something." I paused, and there was silence between us for a few moments. "Did you ever think Daddy might have a drinking problem?"

"I only saw him out of control three times," she answered. "Three times in forty years." Her voice was clear and strong, adult to adult. "He told me once that he appreciated my willingness to drink with him. . . . Why are you asking? Are you concerned your boys might have inherited something?"

"No. I'm asking because your drinking, yours and Daddy's, was a problem for me."

"It must have been awful," she said in her strong adult voice.

"Yes," I said. "It was."

She did not ask me to tell her just how awful it was.

In the thirty-seven years I knew him, I saw my father "out of control" many more times than three, if you consider crossed eyes, a shit-eating grin, mumbling speech, and a stumbling gait "out of control." One night when I was home from college on vacation, I heard his voice from their bedroom, so shrill it was almost falsetto, yelling at my mother: "Leave me alone! Leave me alone! Leave me alone!" I went in and talked to them and felt pleased afterward that I had helped them to settle down. But the next night I heard him again: "Leave me alone! Leave me alone!" I did nothing.

At Thanksgiving and Christmas and other occasions when the extended family gathered, my father made strong drinks for everyone. Maybe it got worse as I got older; maybe I just noticed it more. I remember the last party we had before my sister died, when I was twenty-two. We sat around a plate-glass table set with sterling silver and platinum-rimmed china. It was my sister's house, and her husband's, but it was my father who made sure everyone got more than enough to drink. As everyone got drunker and drunker—one relative had to rush from the table at one point—we looked through the glass table at our feet on the floor below, and pretended we were in the *Ozzie and Harriet* show. After dinner my father murmured obscene Spanish words—the only Spanish words he knew—to my sister's housekeeper, a middle-aged Mexican Catholic.

At another party, several years after my sister died, the family gathered at my parents' cottage in the mountains. I was needlepointing a peace symbol for them—this was 1970, and they identified themselves with the peace movement and the young radicals of the time. My mother was drinking. Her face seemed to have fallen in on itself, a vortex of emotions. As I pushed my needle through the canvas, my mother, the Esalen veteran, said, "I feel you're trying to keep yourself aloof from us."

It was against the rules in our family for anyone to talk about what was really happening, so I did not say "I don't want to be close to you when you're drunk." Instead I answered, "I just like doing needlepoint," while inside I screamed: "I hate you I hate you I hate you!"

That night I dreamed my mother had a knife and was carving me into pieces, and I had a knife and was carving her into pieces. I woke at dawn, a thrill of terror running through me, and ran out of the house and down the trail to the waterfall. I stood panting beside it, staring into the clear running water and gulping deep breaths of the redwood-scented air as I struggled without hope to escape from my prison of pain and rage.

Dad
Mom
Dad
Mom
Dad
mom
me
John

PART THREE

EARLY EXIT

A 1980s survey found men who regularly drank two or more drinks daily were nearly twice as likely to die before age sixty-five than men who drank twelve or fewer drinks a year.

▲

Just as they are powerless to jam the inner mechanisms that drive a parent to drink, children cannot heal what alcohol destroys. When a parent dies of an alcohol-related condition, children are twice wounded, first by alcohol and then by death. Even with alcoholic parents, it's rare that no parent is better than an alcoholic one.

RUSSELL BAKER

from
Growing Up

When his father died in 1933, Russell Baker was just five years old. He was old enough to remember what alcohol had done to his father. Mostly it contributed to an early death. Although moonshine made him violently ill, Benjamin Baker, a diabetic, continued to drink it. (The newly discovered drug insulin might have prolonged his life, but perhaps news of the miracle drug hadn't reached rural Morrisonville, Virginia.) Abstaining from alcohol could have prolonged his life.

After his father's death, young Baker's mother was left with three children to care for. Leaving the youngest daughter with more affluent relatives, Lucy Elizabeth Baker set out to raise her children right. And she did. Russell Baker's autobiographical notes are impressive and include two Pulitzer Prizes, several books, advanced academic degrees, and a distinguished career in journalism.

In this excerpt, Baker recalls an evening with his family when his father was drinking, the sort of night played out in countless homes on any given day.

During all these years my father was under a sentence of death. In 1918 he had been drafted by the army and discharged after five days with papers stating he had "a physical disability." From his childhood it had been Morrisonville's common knowledge that Benny had "trouble with his kidneys." What the army doctors found is not clear from the records. Maybe they told him the truth—that he had diabetes—but if so he kept their terrible diagnosis a secret. In 1918 insulin was still unknown. As a twenty-year-old diabetic, whether he knew it or not, he was doomed to early death.

The discovery of insulin in 1921 would have lifted that sentence and offered him a long and reasonably healthy life. If he ever learned about insulin, though, he certainly never used it, for the needle required for daily injections was not part of our household goods. Perhaps he didn't know how seriously ill he was, but the state of medicine in Morrisonville must also be allowed for. New medical wonders were slow to reach up the dirt roads of backcountry America. Around Morrisonville grave illness was treated mostly with prayer, and early death was commonplace. Children were carried off by diptheria, scarlet fever, and measles. I heard constantly of people laid low by typhoid or mortally ill with "blood poisoning." Remote from hospitals, people with ruptured appendixes died at home, waiting for the doctor to make a house call.

Since antibiotics lay far in the future, tuberculosis, which we called T.B. or consumption, was almost always fatal. Pneumonia, only slightly less dreaded, took its steady crop for the cemetery each winter. Like croup and whooping cough, it was treated with remedies Ida Rebecca compounded from ancient folk-medicine recipes: reeking mustard plasters, herbal broths, dosings of onion syrup mixed with sugar. Boils and carbuncles were covered with the membrane of a boiled egg to "draw the core" before being lanced with a needle sterilized in a match flame.

When my cousin Lillian stepped barefoot on a rusty nail, my grandmother insisted on treating the puncture by applying a slab of raw bacon. When my cousin Catherine's hand touched a red-hot wood stove, my grandmother seized her arm and with fingertips light as feathers stroked the blistering skin while murmuring an incoherent incantation in a trancelike monotone. Catherine's screaming stopped. "My hand doesn't hurt anymore, Grandma," she said.

This was called powwowing, a form of witch-doctoring still believed in then by the old people around Morrisonville and prescribed on at least one occasion by a local medical man. This doctor, after failing to rid Lillian of a severe facial rash with the tools of science, prescribed a visit to an old woman on the mountain whose powwowing, he said, sometimes cured such rashes. "But don't you ever dare tell anybody I sent you to her," he cautioned. Lillian did not go for the powwow treatment; her rash subsided without help from either science or witchcraft.

Very few people ever saw the inside of a hospital. When my grandfather George had a stroke, he was led into the house and put to bed, and the Red Men sent lodge brothers to sit with him to exercise the curative power of brotherhood. Red Men who failed to report for bedside duty with their stricken brother were fined a dollar for dereliction. Ida Rebecca called upon modern technology to help George. From a mail-order house she ordered a battery-operated galvanic device that applied the stimulation of low-voltage electrical current to his paralyzed limbs.

Morrisonville had not developed the modern disgust with death. It was not treated as an obscenity to be confined in hospitals and "funeral homes." In Morrisonville death was a common part of life. It came for the young as relentlessly as it came for the old. To die antiseptically in a hospital was almost unknown. In Morrisonville death still made house calls. It stopped by the bedside, sat down on the couch right by the parlor window, walked up to people in the fields in broad daylight, surprised them at a bend in the stairway when they were on their way to bed.

Whatever he knew about his ailment, my father made no concessions to it. If anything, he lived a little too intensely, as though determined to make the most of whatever time he was to be allowed. By 1927 he had saved enough money to rent and furnish a small house of his own—the tenant house where grazing cows peered through windows—and there, that August, my sister Doris was born. In 1928 we were back in Morrisonville in a larger house, looking up at Ida Rebecca's porch, and there my second sister was born in January of 1930. They named her Audrey.

Benny's development into "a good family man" was evidence of my mother's success at improving his character. His refusal to forswear moonshine, however, mocked her with the most painful failure of all. After pleasing her with long bouts of sobriety, he often came home from work with the sour smell of whiskey on him and turned violently ill. With diabetes, his drinking was lethal. He paid terribly for whatever pleasure he took from Sam Reever's Mason jars. My mother didn't know about the diabetes; all she knew was that drinking acted like poison on him. When he came home smelling of whiskey, she abused him fiercely in cries loud enough to be heard across the road at Ida Rebecca's. He never shouted back, nor argued, nor attempted to defend himself, but always sat motionless as her anger poured down on his bowed head—sick, contrite, and beaten.

One evening when we waited supper long past his usual arrival time and finally ate without him, he came in while the dishes were being washed. He was smiling and holding something behind his back.

"Where have you been?" my mother asked.

"I bought a present for Doris."

"Do you know what time it is? Supper's been over for hours."

All this in a shout.

Holding his smile in place, trying to ignore her anger, he spoke to Doris. "You want to see what Daddy brought you?"

Doris started toward him. My mother pulled her back.

"Leave that child alone. You're drunk."

Well—and he kept smiling—actually he had taken a drink along the way, but just one—

"Don't lie about it. You're stinking drunk. I can smell it on you."

—had been in town looking for a present for Doris, and run into a man he knew—

"Aren't you ashamed of yourself? Letting your children see you like this? What kind of father are you?"

His smile went now, and he didn't try to answer her. Instead he looked at Doris and held the present in front of him for her to take. It was a box with top folded back to display a set of miniature toy dishes made of tin, little tin plates, little tin saucers, little tin teacups.

"Daddy brought you a set of dishes."

Delighted, Doris reached for the box, but my mother was quicker. Seizing his peace offering, she spoke to him in words awful to me. It wasn't bad enough that he wasted what little money he had on the poison he drank, not bad enough that he was killing himself with liquor, not bad enough that he let his children see him so drunk he could hardly stand up. He had to squander our precious money on a box of tin junk.

In a rage she ran to the kitchen screen door, opened it wide, and flung Doris's present into the darkening twilight. My father dropped onto a chair while I watched this unbelievable waste of brand-new toys. When I turned back to see if he intended to rescue the dishes, I saw that he was just sitting there helplessly.

Doris and I ran out into the gloaming to recover the scattered dishes. While we scrambled on hands and knees groping for tiny cups and saucers, the sounds of my mother's anger poured from the kitchen. When the shouting subsided, I crept back to the door. My father was slumped on the chair, shoulders sagging, head bowed, his forearms resting lifelessly on his thighs in a posture of abject surrender. My mother was still talking, though quietly now.

"For two cents," I heard her say, "I'd take my children out of here tomorrow and go back to my own people."

I sneaked back into the darkness and found Doris and tried to interest myself in the dishes for a while. The screen door banged. My father was silhouetted against the light for an instant, then he came down the steps, walked toward the pear tree, and started vomiting.

JERRY FALWELL

from
The Courage to Change

Jerry Falwell's father was a wealthy bootlegger during Prohibition, a good business for an alcoholic. He provided well for his family, and the children never suffered from his drinking until it ultimately killed him. They never saw the elder Falwell at his worst, since their mother protected them from their drunken father. This kind of secret keeping meant many family friends didn't even know he had a drinking problem until he died of cirrhosis, a drawn-out death seen close up by family.

Falwell has come to terms with his father's alcoholism with considerable empathy and forgiveness and manages to remember good about his childhood. Today he leads a congregation of twenty-two thousand in Lynchburg, Virginia. In 1979 he founded the Moral Majority, a political group that attempts to influence public policy with the beliefs of his church.

My father was a successful businessman. He was about five ten, 210 to 215 pounds, a big, rotund fellow with a bay-window stomach, and very aggressive and volatile. He was very kind to us children and gave us everything. I have a twin brother, Gene, an older brother, Lewis, and an older sister, Virginia. Gene and I are both fifty now. We had an older brother who died last year who was eight years older than Lewis. My father was very considerate to us all, probably gave us too much, lavished things on us—automobiles, money, whatever—without our having to work or assume responsibility to obtain them.

In my first memories of my father, when I was a little boy, he was already drinking quite heavily. He was running the Power Oil Company, the Mary Garden nightclub, and a large motel-restaurant. During Prohibition, he ran a liquor business, illegal moonshine, and sold it to distributors. Though he was well known as a lawbreaker, he never had any trouble over it. Dad made a lot of money selling liquor. Everybody in our town, of course, knew that. We lived in a big house up on a hill, and you could either get your oil or whiskey there or someone would deliver it to you. The nightclub was a very rough place. My father also, back in those days, would stage dogfights and chicken fights. They were all illegal, but they were on our farm and everybody came. They would gather in a big circle, betting. My father never had any problems at all with the law because he was so powerful in the county. It was just part of life. I grew up that way.

In 1931, two years before I was born, my father and his younger brother, Garland, who was quite a wild fellow, quite a reckless guy, had gotten into an extremely violent argument. There was a shoot-out, and my father killed him. There was never any trial over it. It was all in self-defense.

I guess that Garland was in his early twenties. My father would have been thirty-eight. There was quite a range between them. Garland had been in a lot of trouble and actually gone to jail. He had been unmanageable by any member of the family. They couldn't handle him. I don't know all the circumstances of that day, only hearsay. Garland was on drugs. He was wild. Completely out of it. Someone had called the police about his throwing firecrackers next door to our restaurant, right there in the city. It was a neighbor who'd called, but since Father owned the restaurant, Garland thought it was my father who had called. When Dad drove up, I am told, Garland came out of the restaurant with a pistol in each hand, cursing and screaming and yelling at my dad. Dad was very hot-tempered, so he drove to our house immediately, a mile away from there. Mother said she knew he was very upset when he came in. He got the shotgun, .12-gauge double-barreled shotgun, and told my mother he was going back up there to see what Garland was doing. She pleaded with him not to go, but he went anyway. He parked and walked in the door, and Garland came out with his two guns again; Dad shot from the hip. I think Garland was hit in the chest or the neck and was killed instantly. My mother said it was the key incident in my father's life, with which he could not cope.

Nobody was bitter with Dad about it. But that incident precipitated his excessive drinking, and he never stopped. Seventeen years later he was dead from cirrhosis.

I was fifteen when my father died. He didn't believe in hospitals or churches, and he never set foot inside either one. He died at home. Doctors treated him there. Cirrhosis causes your liver to stop working. You swell up and then they tap you, draw off the fluid so many times until you are out. You turn very yellow. Jaundice. I remember, as a boy, watching that.

Three weeks before Dad died a man named Josh Alvis,

now long since dead, had come by the house. I remember his coming in to see Dad a lot toward the end. He spent some time reading the Scriptures to Dad, giving him the biblical plan of salvation, the story of the gospel of Christ. Dad accepted Christ. It was not until years later that I was able to put all the pieces together and connect his conversion experience and his last days on earth with what happened and the way he reacted. The last several weeks of his life, probably three, his language and his attitude were greatly changed. Very little hostility there, I recall. I detected that he was ready to die.

Dad used to come home after a long day, really loaded, yelling and screaming, and upset everything. Mother was never disturbed by it, and because she wasn't, we never paid any attention to it. He never struck any of us. He never hurt his family. He was never violent to us. But very noisy. He'd go to bed early every night and get up at four o'clock every morning. By the time everyone else was up and around, he had long since been at the office. I do remember, about the last five years of his life, that he would sleep a lot because the drinking was beginning to take a real toll on him, to debilitate him and deteriorate his faculties. By that time, my older brother, Lewis, was involved in the business, and things were going on without Dad's personal involvement.

Dad never drank to the point where he couldn't run

his business, but several fifths of whiskey a day were not unusual for him. He got to where it didn't intoxicate him, where you couldn't notice it, except for the smell on his breath.

Dad had made enough money in his life, even while he was drinking heavily, that we never had to do without anything. It was nothing, back in those days, for me, a twelve- to fifteen-year-old kid, to walk around with a hundred dollars in my pocket. To the kids I ran with then, that was a mammoth amount of money. It was nothing unusual for money to be piled up on the table. I'd say, "Dad, you got any money?" And he'd say, "Get your handful." He didn't know what I took. He didn't care. I had an automobile by the time I was twelve. My father gave me one. He signed a driver's application saying I was fifteen.

With the license, I didn't have to stay at home. But I didn't dare bring a girlfriend or anybody refined to the house because Dad was totally unpredictable. I brought a friend into the house one day. Dad was sitting at the table. A fifth of whiskey and a .38 Smith and Wesson were lying on the table. He carried a .38 with him all the time. My dad picked up the gun and said, "Don't move, boy." And he put the gun down to his feet. "I've been trying to kill that fly all day." He shot a hole in the kitchen floor, right between his feet. That was the last time I ever got my friend onto the property. Mother just couldn't believe it.

When Mother saw a storm arising, she would just get us out of the house, just tell us to go. Whenever it was just Dad and Mom, he got quiet, because he knew he would never get a rise out of her. There was no point in starting an argument if it was going to be a one-way street. The only time he would put on a show was when he was really upset and a crowd was there. Mother very wisely would say, "Why don't you find something to do? Go somewhere, play with somebody." We always had something going. I was very active, into everything, and all that fit into Mom's way of handling the problem. She made the situation as harmonious as it could be under the circumstances, but rather than bringing a crowd of buddies to our house, I would hang out in the town where the gang was.

The refrigerator was filled with liquor all the time. Dad usually kept a fifty-five-gallon keg of wine in the basement. Good wine, usually several cases of beer, and always cases of whiskey. The refrigerator would be full of it. He wouldn't have cared if we drank it. We never did. I suppose seeing what it was doing to him, instead of tempting us to drink, caused us to hate it. I have drunk some whiskey and beer in my life, wine as a youngster, just piddling with the guys, just to act big. But I never enjoyed it. Never wanted to do it. I think it was because I saw the bad side of it.

Dad would go to bed very early, and, of course, young people don't go to bed at eight o'clock, so we would have to get out of the house and do things, which we did a lot.

We couldn't say anything. Couldn't knock on doors. Couldn't let the phone ring. That type of thing. He was shielded, protected all the time, and he had enough money that he was never deprived.

I knew a lot of kids at school who probably didn't have the money we had, but they had very happy family relationships. Their parents, family, were all close together. We were always careful to cover up, to pretend we had the same thing, talk about it as if we did. I doubt if any of our friends knew that Dad had a serious drinking problem until he was dead.

We had lots of buddies and friends. We just busied ourselves, staying out of the house, staying away from Dad because the situation was definitely uncontrollable. Very few people in our school knew that he had a problem. We never talked about it, and it was really a well-kept secret inside the family and the business that he was deteriorating and diminishing on a regular basis.

Because of Mother, we always had big Christmases, and Dad would unload any amount of money she wanted to buy things. We got big gifts. Big everything. It was all a part of the guilt complex, I'm sure. Thanksgiving, no matter what, we'd always have a big Thanksgiving dinner. To his credit he would really try, until the last year or two, to be straight for the holidays because people would be coming in. It would usually be late in the evenings before he got a little bit difficult. On holidays he might have a little bit. He drank enough that when he drank a little, you wouldn't know it. As a matter of fact, he had to drink a little to stay steady. He'd sip all day. The big citizens around the area would be in during the day. Everybody who was anybody. Dad would take a little drink here and there throughout the evening until he got ready for bed.

Every morning he'd get up, break two raw eggs, sometimes three, into a glass and swallow them. Very often I would see him mix raw oysters with vinegar, salt, and pepper, and then take the bowl and swallow them. I couldn't imagine anybody drinking raw eggs and oysters. But that was his Maalox, the way he kept his stomach livable. He couldn't eat anything until he had those eggs or oysters, and a little drink after that.

I know that I wished that he would stop, that he would not drink. I saw it getting worse. Yes, sir, I saw him physically going downhill. There was obviously a medical problem. And I saw his personality, his will, weakening. I saw him sleeping more. I saw him coming home during the day. I even saw him a few times at his place of business, when he would have his office locked. When I would go look in the window of the office, he would be asleep on the floor, just taking a nap there.

I think we had more pity than contempt. Because it would be nothing for him, sitting in a chair, to fall asleep in the middle of the day, just fall out of it. Toward the last, he really lost control.

I was so much into life, having the money and not having to work, that I didn't have time to feel neglected or sit down and analyze how bad things were. I have a feeling that if Dad had lived until I was seventeen, eighteen, or twenty, I would have begun to build up those resentments. I think maybe I would have come to the place where I really would have resented what he was doing to my mother. I think my biggest concern, the only thing that gave me any bad feelings toward Dad at all, was his making life so miserable for Mom. She would never leave home. She was very much a homebody. I do recall feeling very strongly about the uncomfortable, miserable conditions Mom was in.

She never took on a martyr's complex. She never retaliated against him, and she worked very hard to prevent our ever resenting him. She never allowed an altercation. She took all the burden on herself. It must have been a tremendous burden, but as a result of it, we don't have any bad memories of being unkind to Dad. She would always tell us, "He just can't keep drinking, he'll stop." She would try to give us a ray of hope. I don't think I ever had any hope that he would stop. I don't think I ever believed what she was saying. He died at the age of fifty-five of cirrhosis of the liver, right in the spring of his life. He was victimized by alcohol.

You Dummy

PART FOUR

IT RUNS IN THE FAMILY

Children of alcoholics are more at risk for alcoholism and other drug abuse than children of nonalcoholics.

▲

Children often inherit more than their mother's eyes or father's nose; they also get an inclination to abuse alcohol. Although the children may grow up swearing they'll never be like their drinking parent, they're usually unable to recognize their own alcoholism.

DREW BARRYMORE

from
Little Girl Lost

Drew Barrymore, the memorable towhead in *E.T.*, followed in the family business when she took up acting. The Barrymore family has been world-famous in theater and movies for more than a century, beginning in England in the Edwardian era and continuing to the present day with Drew Barrymore.

When she had her first drink at age nine, she took up another family tradition—one that went back to her great-great-grandfather.

At age thirteen, Barrymore began to tackle her alcohol and drug problem when she checked into a private treatment center. She took control of her life, got back into acting, and went public with her struggles, appearing on a series of talk shows and magazine interviews.

In the following excerpt from her book *Little Girl Lost*, Drew Barrymore illustrates how alcoholism can pass from generation to generation in an unbroken chain of broken lives.

I think my mom and dad were boyfriend and girlfriend for a couple of years, but they were apart by the time I was born. That's about all I know. Once, I remember, I wondered why they had even bothered to have me if they were already splitting up. But I never asked, and no one ever told me. I guess they wanted to leave it a mystery so I could make up my own story.

Drew's parents' initial meeting happened on a Hollywood movie set many years earlier. Ildyko Jaid Mako was a young, lithe woman of Hungarian descent, an only child who suffered what she terms an unhappy childhood, the result of her parents' divorce. From her girlhood in Pennsylvania, she was consumed by dreams of acting in Hollywood. With the dark, exotic beauty of a model—large, inviting eyes, exquisite cheekbones, and a thick mane of black hair—a charming intelligence, and witty repartee, the odds of making it seemed stacked in her favor. It was no wonder that her first encounter with John Drew Barrymore, Jr., was a memorable one.

At the start of the 1960s, Barrymore was the sort of virile man who cast an entrancing spell over women. He possessed dashing good looks, inherited from his father, the great actor John Barrymore, who was called "the greatest lover of the screen," and there was about him a bohemian charisma, a sense of wild adventure and passion and living for the moment. Having acted in a slew of big-screen films, including *The Sundowners*, *While the City Sleeps*, and *Never Love a Stranger*, Barrymore was something of a movie star himself.

However, Barrymore, a true rapscallion, garnered the most fame from his offscreen adventures. A week after marrying his first wife, actress Cara Williams, he was tossed in jail following a domestic argument. Within several years he had been arrested on several counts of drunk driving, hit-and-run driving, and his unrestrained alcoholism cost him his good standing with Actors' Equity. By 1960, bearded and long-haired, he had fled to Rome, where between marrying and divorcing twenty-three-year-old starlet Gabriella Palazzoli, he seemed to rack up as many arrests as he did B-movie credits.

After a brief period of meditation in India, Barrymore returned to California, ever flamboyant and dangerous at a time when it was hip to be on the edge of what society deemed acceptable. He cast himself as an ascetic, and professed to lead a pious, vegetarian life in the desert while composing poetry and writing screenplays. But Barrymore remained as spontaneous, untamed, and explosive as ever. On March 21, 1972, *The New York Times* reported his arrest for possession of marijuana. It was Barrymore's fourth drug-related arrest since the mid-sixties.

Soon after that latest run-in with the law, Barrymore and Jaid were reacquainted at the Troubadour nightclub, a hip Los Angeles music venue where Jaid waitressed. When romance blossomed, they began living together on the outskirts of West Hollywood and soon married. It was easy to see how Jaid could be mesmerized by Barrymore. Yet their tenure together was a violent one. Like the women before her, Jaid thought she might rehabilitate Barrymore, temper the flame that drove him to drink and drugs. She tried persuading him to enter a treatment program. She tried to convince him to go to therapy. She even tried having his baby. But instead of rehabilitation, she turned into a doormat for his abuse. The more she tried to love him, the more he lashed out at her.

Ethel Barrymore, Drew's great-aunt, once asked, "We who play, who entertain for a few years, what can we leave that will last?" She needn't have worried. The Barrymore family, prominent in entertainment circles since the days of England's George III, has continued almost in spite of itself. Each generation has been blessed with its share of talent, beauty, fame, and intelligence, yet the hallmark of each generation has been a penchant for self-destruction.

In the mid-1800s actress Louisa Lane, who delivered her first lines onstage at age five, married the Irish comedic actor John Drew, a slight, outgoing spirit who fell dead prematurely at thirty-four after a period of excess barroom exploits. "Had he lived to be forty-five, he would have been a great actor," wrote his widow. Their daughter, Georgie, a strikingly beautiful blonde who made her stage debut at fifteen, was swept off her feet several years later by a flashy young British actor whose dapper taste in clothes and stiff, proper accent cultivated an air of charm and polish. His name was Maurice Barrymore.

Married New Year's Eve, 1876, the Barrymores set up housekeeping in New York and established themselves as the most prominent family of the American stage, though Maurice's reputation as a bon vivant reveler, womanizer, and imbiber quickly usurped his chance for greatness. Wobbling home one Sunday morning after a night of carousal, Maurice found his wife heading out the door. "Where are you going, my dear?" he asked.

"I am going to mass," she said, "and you can go to hell."

Their first child, Lionel, was born in 1878, and he was followed a year later by the birth of a daughter, whom they named Ethel, after a character in Maurice's favorite novel, Thackeray's *The Newcomes.* Their third child was born February 15, 1882, and christened John Sidney Barrymore. A bright child, he showed an artistic and athletic flair early on, though with parents who traveled constantly, he developed a wild streak that would lead him in and out of trouble for the rest of his life.

John's mother died when he was eleven, leaving him with precious few memories. He grew up unbridled and wanton, a lad who shared as much distinction in preparatory school for his fondness for brass knuckles, cigarettes, and whiskey as for his academic prowess. By fourteen, he was a chronic drinker; a year later he made his stage debut in a nonspeaking role supporting his father, and at fifteen he was seduced by his beautiful young stepmother, an event that Barrymore biographer John Kobler supposed "profoundly affected his sexual development, engendered conflicting emotions toward his father, and produced a trauma that contributed to his increasing alcoholism."

Although he readily preferred art to acting, Barrymore sustained himself by knocking about the theater on several continents, crisscrossing the Atlantic like a migratory gull, and acquiring the skills that would, by the mid-1920s, inspire critics in London and New York to describe him as the greatest Hamlet of his generation. In 1932, the same year John junior was born, Barrymore senior signed a multimillion-dollar contract spanning two years and ten motion pictures. The result was a string of unparalleled box office successes, including *Grand Hotel*, *State's Attorney*, *Dinner at Eight*, and *Counsellor at Law*, which enshrined Barrymore atop Hollywood.

However, the achievements Barrymore accrued were slowly and painstakingly destroyed by the private demons that had unrelentingly tormented his soul since boyhood. By 1942, a string of four divorces—"bus accidents," Barrymore called them—high living, and rampant alcoholism branded the great actor unhirable. Mortgaged to the hilt, his fifty-five-room mansion stripped of its antiques and paintings, Barrymore was a mere shadow of his former self, who possessed just sixty cents in his pocket when he was delivered to the hospital for the final time. He died on May 29, 1942, at age sixty.

> His funeral, attended by more than two thousand people, included pallbearers W. C. Fields and Louis Mayer, and friends such as Clark Gable, Spencer Tracy, Greta Garbo, Errol Flynn, and George Cukor. The legacy of Barrymore's filmwork is unsurpassed, one of the finest bodies of work ever compiled by an actor. Yet it was not without compromise. Barrymore's legacy as a father might well be among the most negligent. His daughter, Diana, was also a victim of alcoholism, and shortly after the publication of her best-selling biography, *Too Much Too Soon*, she died at age thirty-eight. John junior was ten years old when his father died, and the loss appeared to have left the wayward youngster with an irreparable pain that colored the rest of his life and those around him.

My mom hated going into descriptions of my father, no matter how I pleaded. Of course, I didn't begin to ask her anything until I could talk, but even then I learned that he was a pretty sensitive subject. I'm sure it was very emotional for her to relive everything, or whatever parts she told me about, and so I learned about my father only gradually, in bits and pieces, over the years.

I can remember actually seeing my father only a handful of times, the last time when I was seven years old. By then, of course, I had a pretty good picture of who he was, and why it was dangerous to be around him, but there was still so much that I didn't know. Like I was curious about his and my mom's relationship. And why they had me if they were already broken up and all that stuff.

I was probably ten or eleven years old when I finally summoned the courage to ask my mother about that. It was afternoon, and we had fallen asleep on the couch together while watching TV. Both of us kind of woke up at the same time, feeling drowsy and close, and without giving it any thought, the words just kind of slipped off my tongue, softly and easily.

"Mommy," I asked, "what did Daddy do?"

She looked at me as if she didn't understand.

"I mean, what was one of the big things Daddy did to make you really not want to be with him anymore?"

My mom's eyes widened. She looked surprised. But probably not nearly as surprised as I was when it seemed that she was actually going to answer my question. She took a moment to collect her thoughts, a long moment in which she drew a deep breath. Then she started in a soft voice that I wouldn't have heard if I hadn't been lying right beside her.

"Sweetie, when I was pregnant with you," she purred, "I wanted you so badly. I couldn't imagine wanting anything more than you. I felt so lucky to be pregnant, and I wanted the world to roll out the red carpet for you. I'd dream of what a wonderful life you'd have and of how strong and beautiful you'd be. But it was a battle. Your father thought a baby would solve all of our problems."

"And?" I asked.

"Well," she said hesitantly, "it didn't. He was as bad and as obsessive and as violent as ever. So I left him. I had to. Not just to protect myself, but to protect you too. And that just made him angrier and more resentful."

Then Mom started to cry, and I started crying along with her. She didn't want to continue the story, but I urged her on, begging and pleading that she had to. After a minute or two she dried her tears, and then told me that the rest might be too painful for me.

"No, it's OK, Mom," I said. "I have to hear it."

I guess she felt I was right, but as she began recounting that tale, I realized that she was right too. The rest of the story was painful. Although my dad thought a baby would mend the troubles in his relationship with my mother, it didn't. He was unable to handle the pressure of my mom's pregnancy and showed it when his anger reared its violent head. He raged at her all the time. Then one night, she said, he went berserk and beat her up. He hit her and kicked her in the stomach. I suppose he was trying to make me die inside her. Finally, though, someone heard her cries and came to her rescue and took her to the hospital.

"But we survived," she said. "Both of us survived."

The apartment Jaid brought Drew home to from the hospital was a comfortable one-bedroom duplex in West Hollywood, a middle-class neighborhood populated by an unusual mix of artists, Hasidic Jews, and senior citizens. The sun streamed in from large windows, making the plain furnishings appear brighter than they actually were. Jaid filled her baby daughter's tiny bedroom with a menagerie of stuffed animals, determined that she would have the best of everything she could afford, which wasn't much on her meager income.

Upon Drew's arrival, Jaid temporarily shelved her acting career. A baby, she knew, was not exactly what her agent termed a good career move, considering she was a newly separated, struggling actress who owned good stage credits but still lacked the lucrative work in television and film that would make life easier. Still, a baby was cause to celebrate. Jaid had wanted a child, and motherhood was something she felt deep within her soul. It gave her a biblical feeling, a sense of connection with past generations of her family, and that was good. Yet Jaid had no doubt that raising a child would prove a struggle, and that filled her with doubt and worry.

A look at Jaid, a slight woman of fragile, petite build, gave little to suggest the reservoir of inner strength she possessed. But she was a person who, having made a decision, could stand resolute and immutable. Drew became her sole focus, a solitary, overly protective interest that in retrospect seems to have been a reaction to the destructive, ill-fated union that had produced her. In Drew she would find the love that she couldn't find in her husband, and she would return the sentiment even more so.

It was tough. Jaid's priorities were suddenly changed from auditions and acting workshops to food, toys, diapers, and inoculations—and that cost money. A month after bringing Drew home, Jaid went back to work. She juggled acting jobs with a steady waitressing gig at the Troubadour, relying on a revolving group of baby-sitters to care for Drew while she was away. And when she was away, her thoughts centered on her little girl. What new things was she doing? Did she laugh? Did she sit up? Did she roll over? These little things were big events.

Their duplex hardly seemed big enough for the two of them once Drew began to crawl. She was all over the apartment. In the closets, under the furniture, in the cabinets. And one day she was out on the balcony. It was a hot, sultry summer afternoon and Jaid had left the sliding glass door open, hoping to find a cool breeze in the heavy air. However, what she inadvertently created was a passageway to danger. When Jaid glanced up, a diaper-clad Drew was poking through the wrought-iron restraining bars on the balcony, a scant few inches away from a tragic fall.

That's all Jaid needed to see. With lightning speed she scooped up her baby and decided, then and there, to move to a safer apartment. The following week she signed the lease for a two-bedroom ground-floor apartment located directly across the street from the old place. It was more expensive. But nothing was too good for her daughter.

I was too young to realize it, but my mother worked extremely hard so that I could have nice things. It wasn't because she wanted to. She worked during the day and she worked at night, which meant that even though she didn't like it, I was left with a baby-sitter all the time. What effect that had on me at the time is hard to say. Later on I resented it. I felt abandoned. But as a little baby I don't know that it mattered. Maybe it did. I suppose it did. I've been told that I was a very good baby, real easy and good-spirited. Maybe I just wanted whoever was taking care of me to like me.

It was impossible not to like her. At eleven months Drew was a little bundle of tufted blond hair, dimples, and fat. She had a docile disposition, and she seemed to laugh at everything. She was the picture of a perfect baby. Perhaps, as Jaid hoped, the world would roll out the red carpet for her. "Commercials," Jaid's friends would say. "You should get her into commercials." Jaid wasn't interested. For obvious reasons, she had a rather cynical take on the acting profession.

However, completely unknown to Jaid, a friend of hers snapped a photo of Drew and mailed it to a children's theatrical agent, who liked what she saw and responded right away with the date and time for a job interview. That was nice, a nice compliment. However, Jaid politely declined. She didn't want her daughter in the business, she explained.

No matter. The agent, refusing to take no for an answer, telephoned the friend and begged her to persuade Jaid to change her mind, which she managed to do after a second lengthy phone conversation.

They showed up at the appointed place, a big, empty Hollywood soundstage, and entered the outer waiting room only to find it jam-packed with what seemed like every baby in Los Angeles. "Babies coming out of the walls, the roof, the windows, and the Rolodex," Jaid recalls. "Half of them looked like Winston Churchill, and the other half looked like the Gerber baby. I couldn't imagine how they were going to pick one kid out of that pack." The cramped room was a madhouse. Babies cried, nursed, crawled, kicked, and wet. The wait seemed interminable as each child was individually screened.

Finally, the casting director called Drew's name, and Jaid carried her onto the set. The commercial was for Gainesburgers, and the audition process was a simple one. Drew, like the others, was set down on a large cloth spread out in the middle of this vast room. Then they let in a little white puppy. The child's reaction was studied. If they cried or tried yanking the dog's eyes out, they flunked. And if they just sat there, that, too, was grounds for dismissal. Drew did neither. She laughed when the puppy came running in. Then she stuck out her hand and the puppy licked her. She then started nuzzling the pooch. Suddenly, though for no apparent reason, the tiny dog bit her.

Jaid was stunned, stopped in her tracks. So was everyone else in the room who watched the incident. "You could have dropped a pin it was so silent," Jaid recalls. "The puppy scampered away and Drew just looked up at me. She was surprised too. Then she looked at everyone else in the room. There was something like twenty-five people there, and they were all shocked, probably thinking, 'Oh my God, lawsuit.' Then Drew suddenly threw her head back and started laughing, and everyone was charmed out of their mind. They all broke into applause, and Drew just looked around and beamed. She just drank it up. Oh, boy, was she a little ham."

Before they left, Drew was given the job.

I didn't work again until I was two and a half. I was in a made-for-TV movie, which, I think, is my earliest memory of working. I remember lying on a bed, pretending to be asleep. A man came over to me, picked me up, and then someone yelled, "Cut!"

Oh, yeah, I played a boy in that movie.

Acting wasn't in Jaid's plans for Drew. But her longtime friend, actor-director Stuart Margolin, who costarred with James Garner on the hit television series *The Rockford Files,* was making his film directorial debut with a TV movie called *Suddenly Love,* and he needed to cast the part of a little kid. The movie starred Cindy Williams of *Laverne and Shirley* as the mother of a young boy who begins a new life after her husband drops dead of a heart attack, and Margolin, says Jaid, "didn't want to deal with the unknown quantity of a child actor any more than he had to."

Because Margolin was a friend, Jaid agreed to let her daughter work on the movie. They cut her shoulder-length tresses short to resemble a boy's hair, and that was it. The two-and-a-half-year-old charmer was in heaven. Considering her age, she evidenced an extraordinary ability to concentrate while learning her part. When the camera rolled, she hit her marks perfectly. Her attention never waned. Her most difficult scene, the one where the mother learns her husband has died, called for Drew to run up and comfort her mother by pleading, "Don't cry, Mommy. Please, don't cry." It presented no problem. Drew delivered on the first take. "Even when she was supposed to be asleep, her eyes never fluttered," says Jaid.

Margolin was amazed. Drew's mother was equally impressed. "She understood," Jaid says. "Somehow, at that age, she understood what it was all about." More than that, there was a purpose to Drew's acting. It's easy to underestimate the thinking of a two-year-old, if only for their inability to communicate. Yet by that age the ability to perceive and react to an array of complex emotions, like love and hate, fear and acceptance, is already well developed. So although she was unable to articulate it, there was, Drew understood, a purpose to her acting.

The earliest memory I have of my father isn't pleasant. I was three years old. It was afternoon, and I was wearing a pair of jeans and these cute Mickey Mouse suspenders, a favorite play outfit. My mom and I were standing in the kitchen, doing the laundry. Taking the clothes out of the dryer, folding them into the basket. Stuff like that. I was mostly dancing around the room while my mom did the work. Suddenly the door swung open and there was this man standing there. I yelled, "Daddy!" Even though I didn't know what he looked like, I just automatically knew it was him.

He paused in the doorway, like he was making a dramatic entrance, and I think he said something, but he was so drunk, it was unintelligible. It sounded more like a growl. We stood there, staring at him. I was so excited to see him. I was just coming to the age where I noticed that I didn't have a father like everyone else, and I wanted one. I didn't really know what my dad was like, but I learned real fast.

In a blur of anger he roared into the room and threw my mom down on the ground. Then he turned on me. I didn't know what was happening. I was still excited to see him, still hearing the echo of my gleeful yell, "Daddy!" when he picked me up and threw me into the wall. Luckily, half of my body landed on the big sack of laundry, and I wasn't hurt. But my dad didn't even look back after me. He turned and grabbed a bottle of tequila, shattered a bunch of glasses all over the floor, and then stormed out of the house.

And that was it. That was the first time I remember seeing my dad.

The incident sparked a terrible memory. It occurred long ago, six months before Drew's birth, but still lodged in Jaid's mind like a grotesque image that refused to vanish, an unshakable nightmare. She had made up her mind. She was leaving John. She was going to walk out on him. If she wanted to survive, it was her only option. She'd had enough of the abuse, of his drinking and violence. She wanted to make something out of her life. Besides that, she was pregnant, and whether or not he wanted the child, she did. There was just one question: How would he take it out on her?

That was what frightened her most. He would, she knew, do something.

To her surprise, when Jaid announced that she was walking out, John didn't hit her. Not that the scene was quiet and peaceful. There was a pitched argument, all right. There was plenty of screaming, shaking of fists, and pounding on furniture that rocked their apartment like an earthquake. But what John did was worse than striking her. He issued a threat, Jaid recalls, a threat that caused her to tremble. Between drinks, in a smooth, controlled voice that struck like the terrifying calm before a storm, he simply stated, "If you leave me, if you hurt me by leaving, I'm going to hurt you back by making sure that your child's life is miserable."

Whether or not he consciously intended it, John Barrymore, not unlike his own father, cast a tragic shadow over his little girl. He was a puzzle Drew wasn't able to comprehend, an unfathomable mystery she learned to accept as part of her life. As hard as Jaid tried to keep him at bay, his presence hung over them like a ghostly stir.

I remember one time my grandparents—my mother's mother and father—were visiting, and we were coming back from a nice Chinese dinner. I think it was me who ran out of the car and went to get the hidden key. But when I looked, it was gone. Nobody except the four of us knew where that key was. It would've been impossible to just guess where it was. Someone had to have seen us hide it. Anyway, I just turned, motioned like the key wasn't there, and said, "Well, obviously Dad took it."

"He must've been watching us," someone said.

I guess my mom went and called him, because soon he drove up. It wasn't that we wanted to deal with him, to invite him over or anything. We just didn't want him to have the key. Not under any circumstances. Because then he could come in anytime he wanted, and that was too unsafe. We knew how violent he could be. So he drove up and let us inside, but he wouldn't hand over the key.

That's when my grandfather, who was around seventy,

decided to get the key back. Rather than confront my dad, Grandpa asked if he wanted to get a drink. Well, that was great, and the two of them roared off in my dad's car. A couple of hours later my grandfather walked in, holding the key in his hand so that all of us could see it. I think everyone kind of applauded. But Grandpa didn't take alcohol real well, and he'd obviously had a drink or two. He looked so tired and disgusted. I remember him saying, "Jesus, what a jerk." Then he passed out in a chair.

After the TV movie *Suddenly Love*, Jaid was adamant about Drew not acting anymore. It was simply too hard. Not on Drew—on Jaid. If that was selfish, fine. Jaid barely had enough time to make her own appointments, never mind piling up a full schedule of auditions and shoots for her daughter. That would have only complicated what was already a complicated routine of juggling baby-sitters, doctor appointments, and play groups as well as Jaid's own career. "I was still a young woman with my own ambitions," she says.

Life was in a perpetual state of turmoil. During the day, auditions competed with Drew for attention. At night, the baby-sitter would suddenly cancel a half hour before Jaid was due on the set. Or Drew would be sick, and the baby-sitter wouldn't take her. Jaid often found her own interests pitted against her daughter's. She wanted a career, yet she also wanted what was best for Drew, and it was difficult for her to swallow the aspirations she had harbored since girlhood.

"But everything in my life had to serve Drew," she explains. "Every breath had to be for her. I was determined that Drew wouldn't be raised the way I was. In retrospect, I can see the massive overcompensation. But that was my guilt for her not having a father as well as my unwillingness to bring a man into our lives. Drew was Queen of the Hop. She had to be the center, at least as far as I was concerned."

Consequently, when Drew, at four years old, surprised her mother by expressing a well-thought-out ambition with a clarity beyond her years, Jaid found herself taken aback. Not only did she reconsider her position on Drew's acting, but she had to reevaluate her own career as well. The decision turned out to be one that affected their lives for years to come.

A routine had already started. I would complain to my mom about her being gone so often, and she'd say things like, "Drew, just let me go. There are so many bills to pay." I didn't understand. All I knew was that she was leaving me. I felt like I was getting a cold shoulder.

One night she was running out to a play. The babysitter was there, and I had on my nightgown. She was late and didn't want to be delayed by my whining. But I stopped her.

"Mom, I really want to act," I said. "I like it so much."

"I've got to get to the theater," she said. "Mommy's late already. She's got to go."

"But I really want to discuss this," I said. "I really want to act, and I've thought about it a lot."

My mom sat down and plopped me on her lap so that we were looking eye to eye. She decided to get serious with me.

"It's just so hard, Drew," she said. "Look what Mommy goes through. There's a lot of rejection. It's not always like what you've done."

I tried explaining to her that I still wanted to do it.

Out of exasperation she said, "Drew, you just don't understand. It's too hard."

And that was supposed to be that. My mom set me back down on the floor and started to put her coat on. I grabbed ahold of her hand, stopping her so that she'd pay attention to me.

"Mommy, I know it's too hard. That's why I want to do it."

If only for Drew's frankness and serious tone, it was a chilling moment that stopped her mother in her tracks. "I thought, anybody who expresses themselves in that articulate, elegant, and determined manner is obviously quite serious," says Jaid. "Drew just took my breath away when she said that. Mostly because it was so out of context for her age. It was like an older person speaking through her, and I just paid total attention. I said, 'Fine, Drew, if this is really what you want, we'll start something up and see how it goes.' "

However, the one person I didn't give up on was my father. Despite his abusive outbursts, I talked about him all the time. My mom took the brunt of my complaints and anger. I'd always ask her if she couldn't try to make things work with Dad, and she always gave me the same answer: no. Because she left him, I always felt like she was the bad person. At that time I didn't know the situation, and my mother didn't want to depress me by telling me the truth. She accepted the blame while I piled up the resentment.

There were times when I talked of nothing else but my father. I begged to know more about him, to see him, to invite him over for dinner. I forgot about his violent temper. Why was he such a bad guy? I wanted to know. Couldn't I see for myself? When I was very young, my mother thought it was necessary to keep him away from me. But as I became more insistent, she didn't want her resentment of him to get in the way of any potential relationship—if there was going to be one.

Our conversations were always the same. I'd start by telling my mom how much I wanted to see my father.

"But I don't think you're going to be happy with the way he looks," she'd say.

"I don't care, Mommy."

"And I don't think you're going to like the way he treats people," she'd say. "Daddy is not always a nice man."

"Well, I have to learn that for myself."

I was very headstrong, and to my mother's credit, she was accepting of my desire.

So one day I went to my dad's apartment. When my mom dropped me off, I was practically bursting from the excitement and anticipation. I was all gussied up in a sundress, with ribbons dangling from my pigtails, which was a stark contrast to the way my dad looked when he opened the door. He was in tattered jeans and a T-shirt. His shocking white hair hung past his shoulders and he had a big, bushy mustache and goatee. A cigarette dangled from his mouth.

"Dad?" I said, handing him a flower I'd picked outside.

"Come on in, munchkin," he laughed.

What a dump that place was. He had a bed, a cardboard box, and a candle. That was it. He spent all his money on alcohol and drugs, I guess. For the next few hours, while he rambled on about everything from the Barrymore family to Buddha and meditation, I tried to make his place a little nicer. I made curtains out of paper towels and dusted and found a cup to hold the flowers I'd picked. Time must've passed quickly, because what I remember next is my mom honking from the car. Just before I left, my dad went over to this pile of boxes, rummaged through a bunch of junk, and pulled out a white stuffed bear.

"What do you want to name it?" he said.

"I don't know."

"How about Yogi Bear?" he said, handing it to me.

I practically melted right there. When he gave me Yogi, I thought it was like God's personal gift to me. As far as I remembered, that was the first nice thing my dad had ever done for me, and I skipped out of there feeling like the luckiest girl in the world.

Of course, it didn't last. Not too long after, perhaps a few months later, my mom was stuck for a baby-sitter, and she decided to let my dad try it. He'd been pestering for a chance. But she didn't trust him alone with me. No way. So she arranged for her friend Carol to stay over too. We went and picked up my dad, who was acting really drunk, and before we even got home, a fight erupted and my mom booted him out of the car.

She was always tough with him. It was a side to her that I rarely saw. They'd be arguing and all of a sudden he'd say something like "I've got to go. I'm late for a doctor's appointment." She'd roll her eyes and say, "Yeah, Dr. Cuervo, right?" She called him on all his bullshit.

Anyway, he walked the rest of the way to our house, determined to be my baby-sitter. My mom left after Carol arrived, and she went into my mom's bedroom, where she made phone calls, leaving me and my dad alone. We turned on the TV and started talking, and, like always, he got kind of weird. He turned off the lights and lit a bunch of candles. At the time he was hanging around with David Carradine, who had worked on the series *Kung Fu*, and he was real into that karate stuff. For some reason he started showing me how to do the kicks. He'd whip around and, *bam*, snap a kick at me. Most of the time he'd just miss, but sometimes he'd hit me. In the arm, the stomach, the head. He didn't seem to care that it hurt. But I wouldn't cry. The more he continued, the more pissed off I got.

"Why do you always have to cause so much pain?" I asked him.

"What do you mean, little one?" he asked, while continuing to toss off kicks in my direction.

"Why do you always have to cause everyone so much pain?" I screamed. "You're always hurting everyone!"

He stopped and came toward me. There was a crazed sort of look in his eyes. He sat down on the sofa.

"Come over here," he motioned.

Kids don't know any better. So I sat down beside him.

"What do you know about pain?" he challenged.

I didn't know what to say. Then he took my hand and stuck it in the candle flame. It burned and I started to cry. My cries only seemed to make my dad angrier. He let go of my hand and thrust his own hand into the flame, running it back and forth in the fire.

"Don't ever be afraid of fire," he scolded me. "Never be frightened of fire."

He stood up, like he was lecturing me, but I was crying and not listening, holding my burned hand.

"It's all in your mind, Drew," he said.

I heard what he said, but it didn't matter. He was out of his mind. Finally, he drifted off to something else. I think he left the room, probably to go get a drink.

For a time Drew tried to understand her father. It was the only way she could attempt to reconcile her yearning for love and approval and his utter refusal to give it.

"How come Daddy's like he is?" I asked my mom.

Jaid didn't really have a good answer. She explained to Drew that her father had never been loved by his parents, especially by his own father, a man whose affection and approval he desperately craved. John, in fact, had once told his ex-wife that he had seen his own father for only one day, and that the senior Barrymore had been drunk the whole time.

"So your dad didn't ever learn how to love other people," Jaid offered to Drew.

She tried to understand. Nonetheless, the pain of abandonment was woven into the fabric of daily routines and accepted as part of the overall design of life. The lines uttered by Drew and Jaid were spoken so many times, they sounded like dialogue they were rehearsing for a play. "Mom," Drew would say, "do you have to go to work today?"

"Yes, honey, I have to go to work."

"But couldn't you stay home, just this once?"

"We've got bills, Drew. Mommy's got her career."

"Can't they wait?"

"Oh, come on, honey, gimme a break."

Gimme a break. "I heard that a lot," says Drew. At six years old, the only break she could afford to give her mother was silence. She wouldn't complain. She wouldn't tug on her mother's dress as she was getting ready to leave for work. She wouldn't argue. Drew would keep the frustrations to herself, just like her mother contained her frustrations, and she'd simply cope the best way she could.

Drew's recourse was to develop a magnetic, ingratiating charm and a fertile, unbridled imagination into which she could comfortably disappear from reality. The drawings she carried home from school and taped to the refrigerator were full of children playing amid flowers, rainbows, and hearts that floated in the blue sky like billowy clouds. At home she played all kinds of make-believe games with her baby-sitter, and when her mother returned home at night, Drew excitedly recounted her adventures with rock bands, dragons, and movie stars.

Drew especially treasured those cozy nights when her mother was home in time to read her a bedtime story. Over time, they pored through classics like *James and the Giant Peach*, *A Wrinkle in Time*, *Eloise*, and *Charlie and the Chocolate Factory*. One evening her mother brought home a new story, a script, and with Drew under the covers, she began reading a heartwarming fairy tale about love and life and concerning a sweet alien who's been left behind in a California suburb by his fellow extraterrestrials and the little boy who comes to his aid.

I loved it. It sounds stupid, like a cliché, but I cried and I laughed and at the end, I got a real warm spot in my heart. I mean, how could you not?

Two weeks before she listened to this fable, Drew was among the one hundred children who auditioned for Steven

Spielberg's latest movie, *Poltergeist.* However, he asked Jaid if she could bring her daughter back to audition for another film he was directing himself. It was called *E.T.* In Drew, Spielberg spotted the pluck and cuteness he was looking for in the part of the little sister, Gertie. Drew's second interview, Jaid remembers, "seemed to last an unusually long time."

ANONYMOUS

from
The Seattle Times

The author of this piece is a member of Adult Children of Alcoholics. Because this self-help group encourages its members to remain anonymous, she received no byline for her story, which first appeared in *The Seattle Times.* In this piece, she writes of the devastating effect alcohol and drug abuse had on her father. And she shows how his alcoholism endangered her entire family.

A week after my father's death, my mother finally told me about his alcoholism, ending forty years of silence on the subject.

It was a warm spring day in 1984. The funeral was over, the relatives had departed. We had buried my father in a flat plot of ground on the edge of town, a spot where the wind seems to blow perpetually. He had lived a reasonably long life—seventy-five years. Today it still amazes and confounds me to realize how little I know about it.

My mother and I were taking a drive along an old, familiar route—the road to my grandmother's house. It had taken us through soybean, cotton, and rice fields, along a ridge that runs north and south. The ridge constitutes the only high spot for miles around, until the road snakes up into low hills and the square of a small town.

We stopped in a drugstore on the square. "He used to like to stop in here," my mother said. My dad was a pharmacist. He liked to check out the competition.

She bought a cup of coffee; I bought a cherry Coke and a postcard.

Since I have moved away from home, I have become smitten with collecting images of it. This one was a beauty, an archetypal view of an old, rural way of life. On the postcard, about a dozen country people stand in the middle of a cotton field, sacks slung over their shoulders. They look up from a hard day's work in the field. One wears a straw hat against the blazing sun, which lights up puffy white clouds that in July and August never give rain. The card is hand-tinted—the soft, muted colors of the past.

We got in the car and headed through the greening fields for home. My mother began talking as if there were no tomorrow, talking as she never has, before or since. She had spent five years nursing my father through Parkinson's disease and Alzheimer's disease. She was due for some release.

She said drinking and taking drugs had ruined my father's brain.

I must have looked astonished. My father seemed to me to be the meekest, mildest, most inoffensive man who had ever lived. He sat in the same spot at church every Sunday. He was on the church's board of directors. He must have been the softest touch alive when it came to getting people to pay their bills.

My astonishment was short-lived.

My mother reminded me of another drive, my senior year in high school. "Don't you remember," she said, "that time before school when we had to drive down and get him? His boss called and said, 'Come get him' (my dad was working and living in another town, five days a week). We left before school started Monday morning. We picked him up. I think that's when he hit bottom. He never took another drink."

Well, I guess I did remember, though I had been trying for fifteen years to forget. It felt good to remember. A happy ending, right? He never touched another drop.

Except that it didn't end there. My mother, who shouldered most of the responsibility in our family, was rewarded with five years of nursing an invalid who, in all probability, did help his brain self-destruct. After forty years of marriage, my father grew to not recognize his own wife. He developed the disconcerting habit of looking her in the face and saying, "Who is this strange woman? Someone get her out of this house and call my wife!"

My mother and I have a cordial but often distant relationship. After weeks and months of "How are you?" and "How's the weather?" we can suddenly turn on each other like mortal enemies. After years of living with her anger, I still am at a loss to understand it—nor she mine.

For many years, I thought my sister—older, wiser, prettier, and more serene than me—had escaped the unhappiness that seemed to hang over our house like a damp, clinging fog. As we got older, we began to talk. She told me how one of her beautiful, smart daughters had confronted her one day in a teenage rage. "Isn't anyone in this family ever *happy?*" she cried.

My father was a man with a family disposition for alcohol so powerful that he and his four brothers died of it, either through alcohol-related physical problems or suicide. He was raised in a culture where the consumption of alcohol was revered as a sign of masculinity, but where alcoholism was a sin.

In my family are some of the nicest, most charming, sincere, and well-intentioned people you'll ever hope to meet. Churchgoing people. Volunteers. "A" students. Junior class favorites. Queens of the prom.

Except that we live with a legacy of mistrust, second-guessing and depression, born of all the years we lived with what alcoholism experts call "the elephant in the living room." It is a metaphor for the gigantic problem no one wants to talk about, the one that no one will even name.

I have tried to get away from the elephant—although an elephant (Dumbo comes to mind) seems entirely too benign. To my mind, a big, black, staggering dog would be a better fit. I flew away from my childhood, hoping to escape the peculiar dread that living with alcoholism spawns. I forgot many good things about my father—including, I fear, the fact that I loved him.

I am luckier than my father was, I think. I live in an era where people have gotten a little smarter about the effect of alcohol on families.

According to the federal government, there are twenty-eight million children of alcoholics in this country. Six million of them are under eighteen, and they live with their parents' compulsive drinking every day. The rest are like me. We have grown up and moved away. But something still seems terribly wrong, and some voice within keeps telling us that it just might be our fault.

Through the "adult children of alcoholics" movement, barely ten years old now, some of us are reexamining our relationships with alcohol, and with our pasts, and its legacy of isolation, depression, and self-blame.

I know a lot of children of alcoholics. According to the Gallup organization, one of every four Americans says someone in his or her family has a drinking problem. What I say here is particular to me, but in talking with others who have lived with an alcoholic parent, the commonalities between my experience and theirs are so similar as to sometimes make me gasp.

As I write this, I have that postcard at hand.

There is a man in it who looks like my father when he was drinking heavily. He is a big man, wearing a straw hat. He has a big beer belly and a shiny face. But he also has a look of openness, of sweetness, and good fellowship toward his friends. It helps me to remember that he really was a good man. That helps. A lot.

THE HERO, THE SCAPEGOAT, THE MASCOT, THE LOST CHILD

My father grew up in a farm family. The most I know about his childhood, which he never talked about, is this: He played basketball and made good grades. After graduation, he went west to attend pharmacy school, no small accomplishment in the depths of the Great Depression.

He came back home, started working in his uncle's drugstore, and met my mother, an equally shy, very bright schoolteacher. They got married. They had two kids. They moved to another small town. My father opened a drugstore in a small town with at least four other drugstores in it.

My father was never a great businessman. He had a hard time making people pay their bills. He worked seven days a week to make a go of it. On weekends my mother would work behind the soda fountain. I thought that was great. I would get to go down to the store, sit behind the marble counter, and be admired by all the old ladies who came in.

My father was a drinker in the 1950s, but I was too young to be much aware of anything except my own discoveries of the world and how it worked. My parents were still relatively young, and there was still a lot of optimism in the air, though my older sister remembers finding liquor bottles stashed in the cabinets, behind the clean, ironed sheets.

My father gained a lot of weight (in the depths of his addiction, he lost it again). I have one memory of a laughing group of adults sitting around a table at my house, drinking Budweiser. I remember the red and blue can, the Gothic arches and type. They gave me a sip of the beer, and like most kids, I hated it. It seemed like a vaguely disreputable thing to do.

But in other respects, things were fine. I was a very bright kid. I learned to read at a young age. I wowed my teachers, who gave me an intelligence test and promptly kicked me up a grade. I had a distinct notion that I was somehow special.

One day in the late 1950s, my mother, father, and I were taking our customary Sunday drive in the country. My sister had gone off to college. My parents, both raised on farms, loved to drive out and mark the progress of the crops in the fields, the bloom of wildflowers: black-eyed Susan and wild rose. It was in November. The cotton had no doubt been harvested; most of the flowers were gone.

Heading back to town, we saw a smudge of black on the horizon. "I wonder what's burning," my father said. "It looks like it's close to the drugstore," said my mother.

It was the drugstore.

My father was burned out. It was right after Thanksgiving. Christmas, as any retailer knows, is the time of year you make most of your money. My father was without income, and was mostly uninsured.

He spent most of that Christmas season walking around, looking into windows frosted with fake snow and hung with silver balls. Whitman's samplers and Evening in Paris perfume were on the display stands of his competitors. A small-town Christmas. Cash registers ringing with Christmas cheer.

Things were so bad that my parents tried to hide how bad they really were. It was like that afternoon the store burned: I never actually saw what was going on. I sat in the backseat of the car, parked around the corner from the fire trucks and the crowd. I could see the smoke billowing up into the bright winter sky. I knelt on the floor behind the backseat, my head down, my fingers in my ears, praying as hard as I could to God that this was not happening, that things would be OK.

I date my family's troubles from that day. I think my father drank too much, but I believe this dose of outrageous fortune pushed him over the edge. I didn't know exactly what was wrong, but something clearly was not right. I kept praying, for months and years afterward. I think I kept hoping for a Frank Capra sort of angel to appear, one who would lead my dad, cloaked like Jimmy Stewart in his long coat and fedora, in from the snowy streets.

In the absence of that angel's imminent appearance, I tried to be very good myself.

Recently, I read a book about daughters of alcoholics. The author, Robert Ackerman, listed these beliefs, among others, that a child of an alcoholic is likely to adopt:

- If I can control everything, I can keep my family from becoming upset.
- If I please everyone, everyone will be happy.
- It is my fault and I am to blame when trouble occurs.

Mental-health experts believe that one reason the children of alcoholics movement took so long to catch on is that most children of alcoholics are "good" people. Unless they are alcoholics themselves, they are not a burden to society. In fact, a lot of them are trying to keep the world from splitting open at the seams. They are teachers, ministers, social workers. Another reason the ACOA (adult children of alcoholics) movement took so long to catch on: So many therapists are children of alcoholics themselves. They spend their careers avoiding their own elephants by trying to help everybody else with theirs.

What do children of alcoholics do to protect themselves?

Some children become heroes, trying to hold it all together. A few become rebels, though their rebellion is likely to show up years later, its chief weapon the inward-turning one of booze. Others become mascots, trying to regain the love of the "lost" parent by being everybody's friend. Still others lose themselves in a world of fantasy.

I was a sort of only child—my sister had left for college by the time I was eight. Only children, say the experts, are likely to try a little of everything.

After the store burned, my father marshaled enough resources to open another store. It was a bare, undercapitalized affair. My mother's innate good humor began to fray. I became an expert at tiptoeing around trouble.

I tried to be a hero. I made straight A's. Anything less was likely to be greeted with chagrin and shame.

I read like a fiend. Three or four large, difficult books

a week. The librarians thought it was really neat, this little girl who carted books home in her bicycle basket. But my mother, who was working full time to keep us in hot dogs and beenie-weenies, could never get me out of my room to help her with the chores.

That old feeling of "specialness" I had took a left turn. I developed the conviction that we were different from other families. A feeling of differentness is characteristic in adolescents, but it seemed as though my family was a little more different than the rest. Everything was a strain. We didn't have as much money as other families, we didn't buy my clothes in the "good" stores, and we didn't belong to the country club (I later learned this was my mother's doing, because the country club served alcohol). My mother seemed reluctant for me to invite my friends over.

I was sad a lot of the time. I wanted to discuss the problems of the world with my friends, who wanted to discuss mostly boys and nail polish. I developed a friendship with a similarly serious little girl, whose mother started knocking back bourbon at four in the afternoon.

At one point, my father was turned down for a loan. I remember fantasizing about saving the day: marching into the bank, passing a line of speechless, awestruck tellers, upbraiding the president (a member of our church), and marching out with the money.

* * *

The very mysterious part of it was that I never saw my father drink. My parents banished social drinking from the house.

One day I was working behind the prescription counter in the drugstore. I pulled open a drawer and found a big black book that looked like a ledger. I opened it. In solemn type across the top page were the words: "Alcoholics Anonymous."

Alcoholics. Anonymous. I had visions of a group of older men (my father was in his fifties by then) huddled around a table, faces covered with big fedora hats, glasses of amber liquid cradled surreptitiously in their hands.

The book said my father was the treasurer. I shut the drawer.

Despite his good intentions in joining the group, his addiction got worse. With a ready supply of every legal drug, my father began to substitute barbiturates for liquor, perhaps in a misguided attempt to quit drinking. He became emotionally, and sometimes physically, catatonic. He would rise in the night and bump into things and fall. My mother would get up and pick him up. I would lie in bed and try not to hear.

My father whipped me but once in his life—the day

in the third grade when I made a C in conduct and a C in math. He never said more than a half-dozen cross words to me. But his addiction put us all in jeopardy. I remember a terrifying day when I was fourteen. We had driven sixty miles over a winding, turning country road to my grandmother's house—the same road my mother and I would take many years later. My grandmother was ill, and my mother stayed on while my father and I began the drive home. My father kept falling asleep at the wheel. He almost killed us by trying to pass cars on the twisting two-lane road.

After a couple of near misses, I said I would take over. I was fourteen. I was just learning to drive, and I had never driven more than two miles—that on a deserted country road. But he gave up the driver's seat and went to sleep. I drove all the way home, hands frozen to the wheel, praying every inch of the way that we would get home alive.

I must say that we put up an admirable front. My mother's salary paid the bills; somehow they got my sister through a private college. We were in church every Sunday, my father in the audience, my mother in the choir.

But in a distinctly un-Christian fashion, I began not to honor my father or mother. I began to believe that my father was either very sick, or very stupid, or just flawed in some awful way that I could not understand. After a couple of episodes in which my mother locked me out of the house, or slapped me because she thought I was whoring around, I began to give her a wide berth, too.

I am not proud of the way I felt about them. I felt, and feel, terribly guilty about it.

I still thought that my mother, in her own cockeyed way, loved me. I was not so sure about anything about my dad.

"One of the major problems of alcoholic fathers," Ackerman writes, " . . . is that they never talked. They communicated very little and developed a feeling in their daughters that their fathers never really 'knew' their daughters. He often lacked parental compassion and was emotionally unavailable. For example, can you count on one hand the number of meaningful father-daughter conversations that you had . . . what kept you hoping?"

I quit hoping. I became a giddy, mindless teenager. I became everybody's friend and did my best to disguise my intellect. The day I found out that I was a National Merit Finalist, I actually prayed they wouldn't announce it. My mother accused me of being a sheep, of always following the flock. Well, bahhhh. I made cheerleader and, in my senior year, went steady with the president of the local high-school fraternity.

He was extremely popular, a hard-drinking, hard-partying ladies' man. He also drank Budweiser—one after another, and another, and another.

Being his girlfriend was more status than I had accrued in my whole life, powerful stuff for a teenage sheep. But something in my mother's face every time I walked out the door sounded some deep, fierce warning bell within me.

I walked out on him one night at a party, where prospective pledges were being rushed by college fraternities. He was drunk as a skunk. He had no interest in talking to me. I felt like a decoration on his Christmas tree.

It was midnight, but to my own sheeplike surprise, I was fully prepared to walk the five miles home. He caught up with me and took me home. We sat under the streetlight. He cried and cried. I had never seen my boyfriend, who had broken almost every bone in his body playing football, cry over anything.

He told me how lonely he was, how his father didn't understand him, demanded unreasonable things of him, how his father yelled awful things at him when he went on a drunk. I looked out the window of the car, into the leaves of an elm tree that had turned white in the streetlight. I could not call up one shred of Christian sympathy. Beyond the light, the stars seemed to be wheeling out of sync with the slow turn of the Earth. Way out there. I felt very far away.

By now, my father had hit bottom and had quit drinking. I had just graduated from high school. Things began to look up for my parents—he was hired back at a drugstore in town, ending the need for the lonely commute. They joined a new, nondrinking country club and took up golf.

As for me, I got the hell out of town. . . .

I left the house and the town I had lived in for eighteen years for college. Except for visits, I never went back.

The children of alcoholics movement is one of the largest self-help groups in the nation, eclipsed only by its progenitor, Alcoholics Anonymous. Dozens of books have been published on the subject. They have sold millions of copies.

I have read several of these books. Most of them have sappy covers—hot pink is the color of preference. About 70 percent of those who come to Adult Children of Alcoholics meetings are women. I guess the marketing experts think pink is an appealing color for us female ACOAs.

If I sound cynical, I'm not. Well, maybe I am. One of the many pieces of good sense these books convey is that children of alcoholics are survivors, and skepticism is a powerful survival tool. Survivors have strengths, the books say. Recognize your pain, but learn to trade on your strengths.

In my case, my relatively miserable childhood had several beneficial effects.

I continued to be an achiever. I continued to make stellar grades through college and two master's programs.

I learned not to let trauma get in my way. I got married and divorced in my twenties, and scarcely let it slow me down. Or so I thought at the time.

I became compassionate—very concerned with righting the world's wrongs. Even a bit of a rebel, working to end the war in Vietnam.

But I managed to sidestep the drug use that took place all around me in the late 1960s and early 1970s. I had friends who ran the gauntlet from marijuana to heroin. In the main, I abstained. Sometimes I thought about why my friends loved to soar, and why I stayed on the ground. I concluded that I hated the feeling of being out of control.

However, in my second round of graduate school, I did discover alcohol.

I had left my husband to go to graduate school in journalism. It was a good school. It graduates some of the best reporters in the field. Some of my former classmates work at *The New York Times*, *The Wall Street Journal*, the *Miami Herald*, the *Philadelphia Inquirer*, papers that set the standard for quality reporting. Some of them have already written books. Others, I'm afraid, are someday going to get killed, for they are the kind of reporter who thinks Cartagena, Colombia, is a great place to be.

I stuck around after graduation to work at the paper in town. I had a wonderful time, with wonderful friends. We were gonzo journalists. We worked together, played together, fell in love with each other.

And did we drink.

It was an afternoon paper. The last deadline was at noon. We went to lunch and drank beer to relax, at a romantic tavern where weathered old men in overalls came in from the country to shoot pool. We sobered up with the tavern's awful coffee. We worked again, then in the evenings we drank again, and sometimes we sobered up again and worked into the wee hours of the morning.

How much did we drink? Sometimes only a couple of beers. Sometimes two or three of us would down an entire bottle of Irish whiskey in one night. I seemed to get close to an inordinate number of sons and daughters of Irish immigrants, a group historically prone to heavy drinking. The drink of preference was a Catholic brand. If you drank the Protestant version, it was a faux pas of major degree.

It was a heady time. It filled the vacuum of a failed marriage. But we were running on the notion that life was always going to be a series of great stories and soulful drunks. Some of us were in danger of running on empty, to fall back on a song of the times.

Since I have begun to study the children of alcoholics phenomenon, I have thought a lot about my relationship with alcohol. I am at high risk for becoming an alcoholic. I believe that for a time, I was psychologically addicted to it.

The best explanation I ever heard for what alcohol does for the human psyche comes from the play *Cat on a Hot Tin Roof* by Tennessee Williams, the noted southern author, playwright, and alcoholic. The failed son, Brick, tries to describe to his wife Maggie why he drinks. He hears a click in his head, he says. When he hears that click, all pain ceases.

I heard that click. All the pain, the self-doubt, the emotional residue of a failed marriage—and beyond all that, the nagging feeling that something was terribly wrong, though I never knew quite what—washed out of my body and into some spiritual shunt.

Janet Woititz, a founder of the children of alcoholics movement, says one reason children of alcoholics are so prone to alcoholism is that it helps wash the bad feelings away. "When they drink," she writes, "they aren't so serious. . . . For those stuck in unhealthy patterns, alcohol may be the only thing that can provide relief."

That phase of my life helps me understand where my father was all those nights when his body was in the easy chair but his soul was somewhere far away. I understand it, but now I watch the beers I drink a little like a soldier watches a grenade with the pin halfway in, halfway out.

Five years later, our band of merry men and women had scattered, flung to newspapers in the far corners of the country. I wound up in Seattle. A year after I arrived, my father's long struggle with living ceased. And as they tend to do when an alcoholic parent dies, the shadows flitting over my own soul started flying home to roost.

DON'T TALK, DON'T TRUST, DON'T FEEL

I hit Seattle about the same time I hit thirty. It was time to get serious about life, I thought, find a permanent relationship, settle down.

Except that I felt like some kind of shell was forming over my soul. Formerly almost gullibly open to relationships, to new people and friends, I became very, very suspicious of people. I accused selected friends and coworkers of letting me down. I seemed to go after men that I couldn't have. I seemed to be asking something of people that they just didn't know how to give.

I was trying to grow up, finally, and I had nothing to go on, for adulthood had been painted as a fairly miserable place to be. I began to feel cornered. For a while, I tried to blame it all on the Seattle weather, but that line of reasoning kind of ran its course.

My father died. I felt like I was drifting, borne on a sad wind. I thought about going home, to try to shorten the extreme distance that had developed between me and my mother.

One day, after hitting a particularly shattering series of relationship reefs, a particularly nice man asked me out. It was a rainy Sunday evening. We went out and ate Creole food. We went to see a movie called *Stranger*

Than Paradise. He had a cold, took me home early, and didn't kiss me good night. Oh, well, I thought, falling back on a song of the times—another one bites the dust.

Except that he did call back. Six months later, I began to feel the same feeling I had always had in relationships—a profound urge to leave. I decided to try something different. I checked into a counselor. Unlike the other two counselors I had gone to, this one was a woman. Maybe because she was a very good counselor, or maybe because she was a woman, or maybe both, I seemed to be able to trust her. We, and the relationship, endured.

Last year, my boss, who is the child of an alcoholic, started bugging me to do a story on children of alcoholics. I really had no intention of doing a story on something so close to home, but one weekend I took home a book and some articles about the phenomenon and started reading them. In one article was one of those checklists that I hate, the ones that run in *Reader's Digest* articles, the ones that say if you check ten out of fifteen boxes, you probably secretly long to be a grave robber.

Well, I say I hate them, but I usually fill them out. I scored fourteen out of sixteen on this one (I don't lie and I have developed a deep suspicion of immediate gratification). I had the strangest reaction. I felt incredibly relieved. I went out, looked at the sky and started laughing.

* * *

I have started going to ACA meetings (ACOA has become Adult Children Anonymous, opening its meetings to anyone from a family where physical or mental illness, addiction, or any other unresolved problem dominated the home). There are sixty-seven groups in the Puget Sound area, up from sixty-one five months ago. There are groups for lawyers, groups for employees of the Bangor submarine base, groups for gays, and one intriguing group for "free spirits." There is a burgeoning group for Native Americans, its national headquarters at the Seattle Indian Center. They had a convention two years ago. Seventy showed up. Last year, four hundred came.

ACA meetings are kind of like Quaker meetings. People sit in a circle: If you have something on your mind, you say your piece. No one responds; no one criticizes or offers advice. The rationale is that children of alcoholics are notorious fixers—always trying to straighten everyone else's problems to the detriment of attending to their own.

I really resisted this gentle admonition to shut up and just listen. But I think I have realized its wisdom, at least in the beginning of a process that the movement calls recovery. We ACOAs have spent a lifetime hiding what has been impressed upon us as a shameful secret. The first time I said in a meeting, "My father was an alcoholic and drug addict," a flush crept up my face and I almost started crying. But I felt better afterward. I was glad no one patted me on the back and said, "Oh, it's OK," because it is definitely not OK.

The children of alcoholics movement has turned into a real phenomenon, and there's a certain amount of capitalizing on it going on. Janet Woititz's book was number three on *The New York Times* best-seller list before it ever got mass distribution, an amazing feat considering that people had to special-order it. Now some publishers are developing their own "recovery line" of books. There are even inpatient treatment programs for children and families of alcoholics, where you or your insurance company can pay thousands of dollars for one- or two-week stays. There are great therapists out there, and not-so-great ones. Some people get stuck in their pain. One local therapist, Jane Middleton-Moz, tells about a woman who sat in the front row for thirteen of her workshops in a row. Middleton-Moz finally told her that she had probably heard everything she had to say. Compulsive people can get compulsive about just about anything.

In the end, I guess, a person has to chart his or her own course. One thing I like about the meetings is that they're free. You are encouraged to throw in enough money to keep the coffee on, but that's it.

I think the meetings fulfill a powerful need. One journalist, herself a child of an alcoholic, described it thusly: "Corny and weird as it was, I went back every week. I was desperate, and there was something intoxicating about listening to a whole roomful of people telling the truth." A friend of mine believes the meetings fulfill a spiritual vacuum. "I don't think most people have a spiritual life in this country," he says. "It's an environment where you're not judged for being what you are. We've become such a judgmental society. People look at each other on a superficial, materialistic level. Science and economics are not God."

I don't know how I feel about God. I do know how I feel about forgiveness, an old and often-neglected component of the religion I was brought up in.

One day I read in Robert Ackerman's book that children of alcoholics believe this: "Those who love you the most are those who cause you the most pain." I thought: Doesn't everyone believe that? At that moment, I realized that I had some work to do.

I will never know, finally, why my father was an alcoholic, why he chose to withdraw when he could have been there for me, and for his family. The children of alcoholics movement says you have to get angry, and then you have to grieve. And then you can forgive.

Sometimes I feel really sad about my father. One day, writing this story, I started crying, after almost five years of barely shedding a tear. I think it was when I remembered my father's predilection for visiting drugstores, trading bon mots with his fellow pharmacists, commiserating over the high price of overhead. I remembered how his buddies invariably gathered at the store for coffee in the morning. I remembered how he invariably charged just a nickel a cup. I remembered his delight at new things, his love of people, and his compassion for almost all living things. I guess I felt a little of what I had lost.

Sometimes I still get really angry at him. Sometimes I get really angry at my mother, though she and I stubbornly keep at trying to love each other. Sometimes I get really angry at alcohol and the fact that we are such an uptight society that we seem to need it to become human. Mostly I still get really angry at myself, for a variety of things that I unreasonably expect myself to do something about. Like I said, I have a lot of work to do.

I am tired of being angry. I want to forgive. I want to

remember the good parts and the bad parts, that my family was not perfect, that I am not perfect, that we love and live the best we can.

That my father was a good man. That he just drank too much.

GARY CROSBY

from
Going My Own Way

Gary Crosby, the eldest of Bing and Dixie Lee Crosby's four sons, faced his alcoholism and battles it every day. His mother never did, and it affected the four boys' entire childhood. With his strict father often absent from the home, Crosby and his brothers were captive to their mother's whims and mood changes. One moment she would be warm and loving, planning a family outing, only to change within hours into a cross and harsh figure. As all too often is the case, the next day she remembered nothing, and no one ever mentioned her odd behavior.

Like many children of alcoholics, Crosby developed poor self-esteem and a feeling of guilt about his mother's drinking. He started to think that if only he were "good" enough his mother wouldn't drink. The feelings stayed with him through adulthood. He lacked confidence and turned to alcohol himself.

It wasn't until I was eleven or twelve that I realized Mom drank. When I was very young and she still left the house, sometimes she took me along when she spent the afternoon boozing at a girlfriend's, but I was stashed out of sight in the backyard. During the drive home I would notice how her speech had become so slurred she could hardly talk, but I didn't know why. I figured she just wasn't feeling well again. That's what our nurse told us whenever Mom closed the door behind her and disappeared into her room for the day. "Your mother doesn't feel well right now. She's taking a nap. Don't play too loud or you'll wake her." We didn't have to be told twice. When Mom got like that, we made sure to keep our distance.

When she wasn't sick she could be a pleasure. My brothers and I would tiptoe into her room in the morning, and she would throw her arms around us and motion us to sit on the bed beside her while she sipped her coffee. She would laugh and joke with us and ask us about our plans for the day. If we didn't have to dash off to school, she might think up a special treat, something she knew we'd enjoy.

"Well, how'd you fellas like to go out this afternoon? How about a movie? There's a Roy Rogers over at Westwood. Would you like to do that?"

"Great, Mom. That'd be terrific."

"Fine. Finish up your chores and come see me after lunch. I'll have someone take you."

But a few hours later her mood was likely to have changed completely. By the time we were ready to leave for the theater, she might not even remember what she had told us.

"OK, Mom, we're all set to go."

"Go? Go where?"

"To the movie show."

"What movie show?"

"But, Mom, didn't you say. . . ?"

"No. Don't know what you're talking about. Bullshit. You can't do that. You're staying right here in the house where you belong."

There was no arguing with her, so that was the end of it. I only hoped she wouldn't think to summon me back to her room later on, because then she was certain to be worse. Even when she was three quarters in the bag, she could still feel the reserve in me pulling away.

That would hurt her, then make her angry, and that would set her off yelling and screaming and cursing. I would have to stand there and listen until she was done. If I made a move to edge out the door, she spotted it at once.

"Just a minute! Where the hell do you think you're goin'? I'm not through with you yet! Sit down!"

"Yes, Mom."

When she got to ranting like that, she slurred and mumbled so badly I could barely make sense of her rage. I was able to decipher that somebody was a "no good sonofabitch," but wasn't sure if it was me or someone else. Whoever it was, when she paused in her tirade, stared me straight in the eye, and asked, "Right?" I knew I had better agree with her. "Right, Mom. Right. Right."

Sometimes she ended one of those mumblings with just a question mark and waited for my answer. Then I couldn't fake it. A simple "Right, Mom" wasn't enough, and I didn't know what else to say. That would make her even more furious.

"Jesus Christ, what's a matter with you? You stupid? What? You must be stupid!"

"Yes, Mom, I'm stupid."

I couldn't explain I hadn't understood her. Then she would growl, "What's a matter? You deaf? You're not paying attention to me when I talk to you?" Any answer

I gave was wrong, so stupid was fine. "OK, I'm stupid." At least that didn't get me a whipping.

It didn't take much to bring one on at those moments. The slightest wrong expression or inflection was enough to trigger her wrath. "I told you not to let me hear that tone of voice!" she would yell, ordering me outside to pick a switch off one of the trees.

Yet I could never be sure when that was coming. She might seem to be heading that way, when she would shift gears abruptly and veer in the opposite direction.

"Get 'em all dressed!" she might suddenly shout out the door to Georgie, our nurse. "Kids are all goin' to the Ice Follies. That's it. Get 'em all dressed in their good clothes and take 'em."

One time she stopped cold in the middle of a harangue and decreed that we had to learn tennis. "I know what you need. *A sport you can play with decent people later in life*. Georgie, call up the tennis pro. Kids are gonna take lessons!" And for the next few months that's what we did, two afternoons a week.

Often, when I saw her the next morning it was as if nothing had happened. I would sidle into her room expecting the worst and be greeted with outstretched arms and a radiant smile.

"Aw, honey, how are you? It's so good to see you. Come over here and let me give you a hug."

She was all gentleness and warmth then and didn't seem to remember anything at all about how she had raged and cursed and maybe even worked me over less than twenty-four hours before. I think that frightened me even more than the yelling and whipping.

Making my way to her bed, I would go through the motions of returning her affection and hold up my end of the conversation with as much naturalness as I could simulate. But I wasn't that trusting. I still remembered, even if she didn't. It would take me two or three days to stop flinching. And just about the time I began to open up to her again, she would fall sick again and turn back into that other person.

I could never be sure where I stood with her, so I had to learn to read her quickly. At the first sign of a slur I tried to get out of her way, go someplace, hide out. I constantly tested the wind. When I came back in the house, I listened for voices and watched the help, pumping them with questions to find out what sort of mood she was in. "How's Mom?" I would ask. "How's it going? Is she feeling OK?" It was a relief to hear, "Oh, she's fine today, just fine." But I still kept my guard up. There were moments when she was loving and funny and marvelous to be with, but those moments were sure to end.

I had no idea what was wrong with her, but whatever

it was seemed to grow progressively worse. By the time I was nine or ten, the good moments early in the day had all but vanished. She was sick a lot more, and the sickness was making her act stranger and stranger.

One night, as my brothers and I were getting ready for bed, she burst into our room and began flailing away at us while she ranted about something or other we had done wrong. Dad heard the commotion and rushed in a minute later. Without speaking a word, he pried her loose, scooped her up in his arms, and carried her off. That was the last we saw of either of them that night, and there was no mention of it the next morning.

Another morning I came into her room and discovered her sprawled out, unconscious, on the floor of her dressing area. Everything there—the counter, the drawers, the walls—was mirrored glass, and her motionless body reflected into infinity. She must have passed out while sitting at her dressing table and tumbled off the stool. But I still didn't know about drinking and passing out. I only knew she was far sicker than she had ever been before. Maybe she was dead.

I went screaming off to Georgie in terror.

"Georgie! Help! Come quick! Mom's sick or something! She's lyin' on the floor in there!"

Georgie hurried to her and immediately took charge.

"It's all right, Gary. Don't worry about a thing. Go

downstairs. I'll see you in a few minutes."

Miraculously, an hour later Mom was up and about again. But I had to wonder, "What kind of sickness is this? And why doesn't the doctor make her better?"

It was an enormous relief to discover that the trouble with Mom was booze. At least that made some sense out of her illness.

I figured it out from watching the parties at the house. Every so often, when Dad was between pictures and didn't take off out of town, he would have a few dozen people over for the evening. By the standards of Hollywood entertaining, they were just casual little get-togethers. The men wore neckties, and the women put on their jewelry and furs, but there were no tuxedos or evening gowns or heavyweight producers who might do Dad some good. The guests were mostly friends in the business who were fun. Some were stars, like Bob Hope and Judy Garland, but there were also propmen, stunt men, songwriters, second leads, and a good assortment of the show-business characters Dad enjoyed.

About the time they got into their first drinks and hors d'oeuvres, my brothers and I were shipped off to bed. But if Georgie wasn't standing guard, we would sneak down the long hall from our room, hang over the banister at the top of the stairway, and spy down on them as they laughed, sang around the piano, and swapped stories about the old days. By the peak of the evening, the serious drinkers would have gotten themselves thoroughly loaded. That's how I made the connection. One night I finally figured out that when Mom became sick she was just like them. There was the same slurred speech, the same peculiar expression on her face, the same strange behavior, so that's what it had to be. That ended my confusion and dispelled most of my fear. As long as I knew what it was, I could more or less handle it.

My brothers assimilated the knowledge about the same time. We didn't talk about it, but we didn't have to. I don't recall ever discussing it with Dad either. The closest he came to directly acknowledging Mom had a problem was that night he stopped her from whacking on us and carried her back to her room. Yet we knew that he knew, and somewhere along the line he figured out that we did, too. When he returned home from a trip, he would ask us, "How's your mother been?" I would answer, "OK" or "Well, she was good for some of the time and not too good for the rest." That ended the discussion, but each of us was perfectly aware of what the other was saying.

Dad was away a lot those years. If he wasn't making

movies and records and doing his radio show, he was touring military bases, playing war-bond rallies, or off with his cronies on hunting and fishing trips and golf excursions. We didn't see that much of him, which was all right with me. I thought of him as God Almighty, the Great Circuit Court Judge. It seemed to me that he came into town just to pass judgment on all the bad things we had done; then he would punish us and go off again.

I always breathed more easily when he packed up his bags and golf clubs and left for a while. It meant there was one less person to mete out punishment, another pair of eyes that wouldn't be scrutinizing me to find something wrong. And when he was away, Mom might start hitting the bottle early and be in bed for the night by the time I got back from school. Then I wouldn't have to face either of them. There was still Georgie, their surrogate when they weren't around, but she couldn't keep up with all four of us all of the time. It's a terrible thing to say, but I liked it better around the house when Mom was drinking and passing out early and Dad was gone.

Two or three days before he was due home, Mom would try to straighten up and pull herself together. But that's no time at all to dry out, and it would leave her in a state of whoops and jingles. Her nerves were so raw that the slightest wayward look or comment was enough to throw her into a black depression, and she would jump right back into the jug again.

Mom's drinking must have mystified the old man. To his way of thinking, everyone had the strength to do anything, so it was simply a matter of wanting to stop. From the stories I heard years later, that's what he did early in his career when he was well on the way to the same problem. Evidently he was quite the carouser when he sang with Paul Whiteman's band in the late twenties, and the heavy partying took its toll on his work. That's supposed to be why Whiteman fired him. Yet shortly after he married Mom he decided to turn it off, and that was the end of it. When she wasn't able to do that, I'm certain he didn't know what to think.

Part of Mom did want to stop. She had a Freudian psychiatrist, Dr. Tony Sturdevant, come to the house to work with her, and he did manage to help her somewhat. There were weeks and even months when she didn't touch a single scotch. But sooner or later she invariably went back to it. Dad had to be beside himself when he realized the doctor wasn't able to fix her up for good. I can imagine his frustration. "Jesus Christ," he must have said to himself, "what the hell am I paying him all this money for if he just keeps coming here and nothing gets any better?" I don't know if the doctor ever could make him understand why she was having such a hard time. Dad knew a lot about a lot of things, but he didn't have much feeling for psychological complexities and for how dark and fearsome life can sometimes seem.

I remember his response, a few years before he died, when one of my brothers flew off into the manic phase of the manic-depression that bedeviled him. I was trying to explain why his son was under sedation in the hospital when he stopped me in midsentence, stared me straight in the eye, and asked in all sincerity, "Tell me something, Gary. How the hell does anybody have a mental problem? What's that about?" Mental problems were all around him. I had them. My brothers had them. His own wife had them. But he was so strong and self-assured and so blessed in his professional life that they remained beyond his comprehension. I didn't know what to answer. I simply said, "Well, I guess everybody ain't as strong as you are, Dad. That must be it." He threw me a funny look, shook his head, and changed the subject.

At times Dad ran out of patience with Mom's boozing, and I would hear their voices rising and falling in anger down the hall. They did their scrapping in private and attempted to keep it cool in front of the kids. When Mom was in an especially bad way, she might slip a little and let out eight bars at the old man while we stood within earshot. But her mutterings were largely unintelligible, and the moment she started we automatically excused ourselves and beat it out of the room. I tried not to listen in on their arguments, partly because I didn't want to hear them and partly because I was afraid of being caught. There were too many people working around the house. God help me if one of them found me eavesdropping and decided to turn me in.

If I accidentally surprised them in the middle of a quarrel, they threw up an instant cover. One evening I rounded the corner into the den and found them going at it full blast. I slammed on the brakes but was already too far into the room to back out. Yet they straightened up on the spot and, almost in unison, began firing questions in my direction about how I had done at school that day. Put on the defensive, I forgot about everything except what I could safely tell them and what I had better keep hidden. It wasn't until they were through with me and sent me off to my room that I realized what I had witnessed.

Most of the time I knew they were angry with each other only because they seemed more distant than usual and particularly formal and polite.

In public they made a special point of presenting a united front. When friends came to the house, or on the rare occasions when they went out together, it would be impossible to tell they weren't getting along. There was never a cross word. They did a hell of an act.

Dad and Dr. Sturdevant weren't the only ones who tried to get Mom to stop. From time to time some of her women friends also took a shot at it. Mom had two sets of girlfriends. They could be divided neatly into those who drank and those who didn't. The drinkers were mostly the wives of stars and other men in the business. They would hit our house late in the morning and spend the day in her room or the den gossiping and laughing while they slugged it down. Many of them were bright, beautiful, funny women who seemed to have everything, yet all they liked to do was go to someone's home and get loaded. I couldn't understand why. By five o'clock they would be gone. Even when they were completely bombed, they still had enough wits to take off before Dad came home.

The other, smaller group consisted of friends from the old days before Mom was married, women like Pauline Weislow, who had gone to high school with her, and Alice Ross, her pal from the years when she was still making movies. Mom usually didn't drink as much when they came to visit. When she did, they might risk her ire by saying something about it. They wouldn't come right out and flatly tell her, "Dixie, don't drink." No one except maybe my father talked to her like that. But as the afternoon wore on and they watched her become more and more wasted, she would read the unhappiness on their faces and call them on it.

"What's a matter with you?"

"Well, gee, Dixie, you know. Why don't you lighten up on that stuff?"

Not that the suggestion did much good. It just put her on the defensive.

"You don't tell me what to do. I'll live my life, you live yours. You want to drink, you can drink. You don't want to drink, you don't have to drink. If I feel like drinking, I'm gonna drink."

There was nothing more to be said, so they backed off until the next time. But they loved her in spite of it. They never let their disapproval build to the point where they stopped coming around. And she loved them, too—better, I think, than her drinking buddies. At least they showed they cared about her. And Mom appreciated that, even though she knew they weren't ever going to make her change.

Grandpa Wyatt didn't know what to do about her either. Her boozing must have broken his heart. Mom was the only one of his children still alive. His other two daughters had both died of rheumatic fever. His wife, Nonie, was on the way out, too, so Mom was about all he had left.

She hated for him to see her when she was in her cups. It made her too guilty. But when she was on a long binge, it couldn't be avoided. She didn't try to hide what she was up to. She drank in front of him. It had to make him crazy. I'm certain they fought about it. Knowing Gramps, he wouldn't let that slide by for a second.

Georgie loved Mom, too. I remember her as a short, stocky, fanatically devout Irish Catholic with a Boston accent, wiry hair, and a grim face. She was hired on as our nurse when I was about eight and quickly became the lord high executioner of all my mother's rules. The instant one was broken she went running off to Mom or, more and more frequently, took care of the punishment herself by going after us with wire coat hangers. Georgie was bound and determined that Mom's commandments be carried out to the letter. She ran us out of the kitchen so we wouldn't hang out with the help, whacked us when she caught us whispering in bed in the morning, forced us into Mom's bedroom to say hello when we came back from school, even though we tried every ruse in the book to keep away because of our fear about what we might find. Georgie never would admit

Mom drank. According to her, some days she just didn't feel well. Through all this Georgie kept saying how much she loved us, which made me really wonder what love was all about.

After a while Georgie took over the running of the entire house, acting as my mother's voice when Mom withdrew into her room and wouldn't see anyone else. If the hallway had to be cleared, the floors scrubbed and waxed or the car taken to the garage, Georgie was the one who delivered the orders, then stayed on top of the staff to make sure it happened. She did the work of two or three people—all out of love. Her devotion to Mom was so complete that she had no life of her own and didn't seem to want one. When the time came for her vacation, she wouldn't know what to do with it. I don't believe she ever took a day off. She was a middle-aged woman, years older than my mother, but it was almost as if she were her daughter.

When Mom was on a heavy bender, Georgie vanished into her room and played backgammon with her for days on end. They played through the night without stopping. In the morning she reappeared long enough to pack us off to school and get the house running, then went back inside and continued the game. Sometimes Mom yelled and hollered at her, but Georgie took almost any abuse she heaped on her without a complaint.

One afternoon when Mom was in an especially bad way, she became so frenzied about how Georgie had played a double six that she picked up a shoe and hurled it at her, smashing her hard on the face. But Georgie kept on playing.

Every great once in a while she stomached as much as she could bear and threatened to leave.

"That's it! I'm quitting! I'm getting out of here! I can't take it anymore!"

But all Mom had to do to turn her around was apologize.

"Aw, come on, Georgie. I'm sorry."

"Well, OK."

Then they went right back to the backgammon board.

God never created a more perfect partner for an alcoholic.

I'm not really sure when my mother started drinking. One of the earliest memories I have about anything is the nurse's admonition to play quietly because Mom was feeling sick, so she must have been into it by the time I was four or five. But I'm fairly certain she didn't start until she got together with Dad.

They met in 1930, when he was singing at a nightclub

in Los Angeles, and married before the year ended. Dad was about twenty-nine. Mom was ten years younger but was already becoming established as a featured actress and singer in the movies. The head of Fox had brought her out to California just the year before from New York, where she was playing the lead in *Good News*, singing the hit song of the show, "The Varsity Drag." He signed her to a three-year contract, put her in the Fox *Movietone Follies* of 1929, one of the first talkies, then followed that up with a slew of other musicals and comedies. Some of the pictures starred top performers like Janet Gaynor, Will Rogers, and Clara Bow; others were amiable quickies with titles like *Cheer Up and Smile*, *The Big Party*, and *Let's Go Places.* In something like a year and a half she made eight of them. Her personal notices were good, and her career was building nicely.

All this happened so fast that her head must have been spinning. When Mom was whisked off to Hollywood, she had been on Broadway all of seven weeks. In typical show-business fairy-tale fashion, she had been called in from the road company when the star fell ill and couldn't go on. The road company job was her first show, and she had been doing it for only five weeks when she moved on to New York. Before that, her professional experience was pretty much limited to singing at the College Inn in Chicago for a month. Her folks had moved there from Tennessee three years earlier, and she was still in high school. The engagement was her prize for winning an amateur contest judged by Ruth Etting. From the stories I've heard, a high school classmate entered her name in the contest without telling her, and either Grandpa Wyatt or Nonie had to talk her into showing up. She was so young and had so little ambition and self-confidence that her agent had to force her on the train to Pittsburgh when he got her her first real job with the road company of *Good News*.

When Mom met my father, he had recently been fired by Paul Whiteman for spending too much time partying and not enough taking care of business. Dad had worked with the Whiteman orchestra for about three years, singing with Harry Barris and his childhood pal Al Rinker as the Rhythm Boys trio. That was his big break, but he seemed to care more for wine and women than he did for song, and Whiteman finally ran out of patience. For a while the trio worked on their own at the Montmartre Café in Los Angeles, then moved over to the Cocoanut Grove, where Dad began to attract a good bit of attention for his solo spots in the act. He was becoming the hot new singer in town to the show-business insiders who patronized the club, but he hadn't yet broken through to a larger audience.

According to a frequently told story, when Mom informed Sol Wurtzel, her boss at Fox, that Dad had proposed to her, the producer shook his head in disapproval and said, "If you marry that Crosby character, you'll have to support him the rest of your life. He'll never amount to anything." The state of their respective careers is summed up nicely by another tale that's been passed along through the years. The headline of the Associated Press release announcing their wedding read DIXIE LEE, FILM ACTRESS, TODAY MARRIED MURRAY CROSEY, ORCHESTRA LEADER, AT A SIMPLE CHURCH CEREMONY.

Supposedly, before Mom consented to marry Dad she made him promise to quit boozing and knuckle down to work. A feature story published in 1952, the year of her death, stated that during their courtship she had launched a one-woman campaign to straighten him out. "She'd break his gin bottles and cart him off to a Turkish bath every time she thought it wise. She laid down pretty strict rules of deportment and was a stern disciplinarian whenever Bing broke them."

The campaign did not succeed until after the wedding day had come and gone. Dad had Sundays and Mondays off from the Cocoanut Grove, and he took to spending his weekends partying at Agua Caliente, a resort just over the Mexican border. Sometimes he got back too wasted to put on much of a show. Sometimes he didn't get back at all. Eventually his boss tried to fine him for missing work, but Dad wouldn't put up with it and quit.

I can only wonder if that was the reason, but right about this time Mom took off by herself and headed down to Ensenada, Mexico. The Associated Press reported the story on March 5, 1931: "Dixie Lee, featured film player, and Bing Crosby, orchestra and radio singer, have separated and she soon will sue for divorce." Mom told the reporter, "We have been married only about six months, but already we have found we are not suited for each other. Our separation is an amicable one."

According to one account, Dad followed her down to Mexico, promised to straighten up, and prevailed upon her to come back to him. Ten days later, on March 15, another Associated Press dispatch reported the reconciliation:

"Dixie Lee's five months' marriage to Bing Crosby seemed short enough when she announced a week ago that they had parted, but they hung up a new record today when it was learned they were reunited. The reconciliation between the crooning member of Gus Arnheim's band and the Fox film comedienne was brought about in the most approved motion picture scenario manner. They just kissed and made up."

From what I've been able to piece together, Dad kept his promise. He didn't exactly join the temperance union, but he did cut back on the heavy partying and began to attack his work more seriously. Putting the Rhythm Boys behind him, he decided to go out on his own and brought in his older brother Everett to guide his new career as a soloist. Everett had been selling trucks in Los Angeles and handling bits and pieces of Dad's business on the side, but now he took over managing him full time.

Dad's career took off almost at once. About six months before the separation, he had gone into the studio with Gus Arnheim's orchestra, which had backed him at the Cocoanut Grove, to record a song written by Harry Barris, his partner in the Rhythm Boys. The tune was "I Surrender, Dear," and when it turned into Dad's first big solo hit, Everett rushed a copy to William Paley, the head of CBS, and sold him on Dad as a radio singer. In the fall of 1931, just half a year after he and Mom reconciled, he began his own national radio show from New York. That November Everett parlayed the program's success into a ten-week appearance at New York's Paramount Theater. The run was extended to an unprecedented twenty-nine weeks at a hefty four grand a week, and Paramount Pictures signed him to star in *The Big Broadcast* of 1932. While he was shooting the movie back in Los Angeles, the studio was so delighted with his work that it grabbed him for five more pictures at sixty thousand dollars a copy. By 1933, the year of my birth, he had already become the Bing Crosby everyone in the world knew and loved.

I don't know if he asked Mom to give up her career when her contract with Fox expired. I doubt whether he had to. For all her feistiness, there was an introverted, painfully shy, and uncertain side to my mother that made performing an agony. She was good at it, but she told me more than once how much she hated it. I saw that for myself some years ago while watching a clip from one of her old movies. At first I just listened to her voice. Her singing was free and effortless and, within the confines of the arrangement, unusually creative. She bent notes and added little embellishments and sounded like she was having a marvelous time. But then I looked up at her image on the screen. Her arms were fixed rigidly at her sides. Her fists were clenched so tight I could almost make out the whites of her knuckles. Her whole body seemed to be screaming, "I am frightened to death."

She had absolutely no confidence in her talent, a trait she passed on to me. When she looked back at her career with reporters, she almost always found a way to put herself down. Reminiscing with Hedda Hopper about the amateur contest that started the whole thing off, she told her, "I was so bad and nervous that Ruth Etting must have known that I was a real amateur. She voted for me." Her recollection of her performance in *Good News* was equally self-deprecating. "The band was hysterical over my dancing. The boys just hoped that I'd do one number right." She talked the same way with Louella Parsons about her movies. "When I was with the old Fox company I made the world's worst picture, *Follies* of 1929. If they didn't know how bad I was—I *did.* I hadn't been so bad on the stage. But I knew a movie career was not for me. When I was right at the height of my flop—Bing and marriage came along."

I'm certain the bullshit of the business also had her climbing the walls. My mother was an outspoken, irreverent woman with a mind of her own. She couldn't endure anyone who wasn't straight and honest. When gossiping with her girlfriends, she saved her most acid barbs for the stars and other high rollers who were overly impressed with themselves. She simply didn't have it in her to go through the ass kissing and false friendships necessary for a young actress trying to build a career. When she found a reason to give it up, she could only have been relieved. Not that she married Dad for that reason. She had to be in love with him. She had to want a home and children and all the rest of it. But marriage also gave her a way out of the jungle.

To this day I don't know what to make of the fact that

she went back to it, however briefly, shortly after Phil and Denny were born. If life at home isn't working out for a married actress, the first thing she's likely to do to salvage her ego is pick up her career and throw herself into work. But even in her most down moments Mom never once mentioned the possibility. On the other hand, maybe she came back when she did just because the first years of marriage were so happy that they made her feel strong enough to handle it. Maybe she thought, "Now that I have love and a husband and a home, it won't be so hard to get out there."

Whatever the reason, in January 1934, when I wasn't quite seven months old, the papers printed the news that she was returning to the movies to costar with Lanny Ross in *Melody in Spring*. The return was postponed, I suppose because she discovered she was pregnant with the twins. But she did make it back a year later in a picture with George Burns and Gracie Allen titled *Love in Bloom*. "Mrs. Bing Crosby has taken Hollywood's biggest risk and decided to combine marriage with a career," the interview proclaimed, and then went on to list all the two-performer marriages that had failed. Mom seemed fully aware of the risk. "Just because a wife has a career," she told the reporter, "is no reason she should lose sympathy for her husband's. This is an experiment in every sense. I'm keeping an open mind about what happens to my home. I think I'll be able to feel which way the matrimonial wind is blowing. And you can bet that if it looks like a squall, Dixie Lee will trim her sails for Mrs. Bing Crosby."

Love in Bloom was trashed as a "complete waste of time," though Mom's personal notices were good. One reviewer thought she gave a "winning performance." Another wrote, "Miss Lee's performance and beauty make up for a lot of things." The results were pretty much the same with the other movie she shot that year, *Redheads on Parade.* The critics treated her kindly, but their response to the picture must have made her think twice about going on. It certainly didn't do her ego much good. And then, after trying it a few times, maybe she found that performing was still murder for her. Maybe Dad also pressured her to quit. Louella seemed to think so. When she announced that Ethel Merman had been brought in to replace Mom in the film of *Anything Goes*, she wrote, "I thought Bing Crosby gave his consent for Dixie Lee to appear opposite him in *Anything Goes* a little bit too easily. He probably realized he could talk her out of it later, and that is just what he has done." In any case, that ended it. In 1935 Mom retired for good and disappeared into the house.

* * *

For all intents and purposes, she was left there. I suppose that's when the heavy drinking began. Not that Dad was entirely to blame for leaving her by herself. Some of it was her fault. He would invite her along on location or to the studio or over to a friend's for the evening, but she always turned him down. By my early teens they had long since settled into a predictable routine where they both just went through the motions of playing out the script. When he came home, he would say, "Hey, there's a thing at seven over at Van Heusen's. Would you like to make it?" She would answer, "Oh, gee, I don't know. I don't think so." And then his line would be, "Well, OK. I'll see you later, 'cause I'm going." That would be the end of it. It was no big thing as far as he was concerned. He had asked, and if she preferred to stay home, well, that was fine. But as soon as he took off, she collapsed into the dumper. And when she was drinking, she vanished into the bottle.

Sometimes the booze made her let down her guard, and I would overhear her grumbling to herself that he never wanted to take her along or do anything together. When I was about seventeen, I started looking at him from that standpoint, asking myself, "Well, does he or doesn't he?" I saw that he always asked and she always refused, so I thought at first, "Well, what the hell is she complaining about?" Then it finally dawned on me that although he made the advances, she wasn't reading them. He would only take one step, and that wasn't enough for her.

Mom was shy. She had to be coaxed. Otherwise she felt she was in the way and was just being asked along out of politeness. Once she was forced into a corner and had to talk with people, she held her own beautifully. She was funny and warm, and everyone loved her. But when it was left up to her, she agonized over leaving the house. What she needed was for Dad to grab her by the arm and tell her in no uncertain terms, "That's it. I'm not listening to any more of this nonsense. You want to go and you know damn well you want to go, so come on, get dressed." But he didn't know how to reach out that far. He didn't recognize her need for constant re-affirmation or recognized it but couldn't give it. He was not a demonstrative man. And Mom couldn't tell him. It would have been impossible for her to sit him down and say, "Look, I'm shy. You have to coax me." So he went out alone, and she stayed home, got depressed, and drank.

Dad wasn't able to express it directly, not face-to-face, but I know he loved her deeply. Mom told me how, when he went out of town, he wrote her long, marvelous love letters that were full of feeling. Yet once he came back, the best he could do was speak to her in a kidding, wisecracking manner from which she was supposed to deduce, "Oh, yeah, Bing loves me. That's just him." But for her that wasn't enough. And that was her problem. I can't attribute it all to him. She needed more affection than most people require. And she did her own job of hiding it. Most of the time she was equally off the cuff with him. When things were bad between them, they hardly spoke at all, but when they were good, they masked their real feelings behind a facade of banter and comic takes.

"Ah, the Romantic Singer of Songs You Love to Hear is home," is how she would greet him when he returned from the studio.

He would break into a tune and sing, "Yes, I'm home, and it's lovely to be here."

"That's marvelous, dear. Just marvelous."

"And what did you do with your day today?" he might ask. "Anything earthshaking happen?"

"Oh, Alice and Pauline dropped by."

"Oh my God, that's wonderful. That's terrific."

"And how was your day?"

"Oh, well, I did the usual thing. I was my usual charming self at all times."

Often, when he came down for breakfast in the morning, they did a few minutes of stand-up comedy on the way he was dressed.

"Mmm, magnificent. Marvelous outfit today."

"Wha-a-at? What's wrong with this?"

"I don't think the yellow socks really show off your blue suit to best advantage, do you?"

"Well, I just thought they were light. I didn't know they were yellow."

"Uh-huh. Well, don't you have a dark pair somewhere up there in your dresser?"

"Why, yes, I think so. I suppose I could rustle one up."

He would go upstairs to change, and when he came back down wearing brown ones, she would shake her head in mock exasperation.

"It's such a good thing that that's part of your image. It's so smart of you to incorporate that in."

On the humorous level they got along fine. Everywhere else the gap between them continued to widen as the years passed. She became increasingly reclusive and drank more. He was gone for longer and longer stretches of time. When he was home, they merely coexisted behind the walls.

More than anything, the picture I have of my mother is that of a rich man's wife sitting around her huge barn of a house by herself. The closest she came to breaking out of her seclusion was during World War II. What with the bond shows and the tours of military bases added on to his other activities, Dad was hardly home at all. Mom's heart went out to the servicemen, too, and she managed to rouse herself from her depression to do something about it. She wasn't a joiner, but on her own she sent a constant flow of checks to hospitals and charities, planted Victory gardens in the backyard, and threw open her doors to anyone in a uniform who was passing through town.

She virtually ran her own Hollywood canteen at the house. She gave the GIs parties, fed them, fixed them up with dates with single women she knew in the business, handed over whatever money she had in her purse if they were broke, lent them her Packard convertible for the evening, and listened to their troubles when they wanted to talk. One badly wounded kid, a paraplegic who got around in a specially built car, visited regularly. He would lift out his wheelchair, then drag himself out with his arms and roll himself up the driveway. He and Mom talked together for hours. I imagine she helped him more than a little.

It's a peculiar thing to say, but the war was a good time for her, in the sense that it made her busy and productive and fired with purpose. She was needed. She could do something for someone. There wasn't much she could do for Dad. He was too self-sufficient. He never seemed down or troubled or frightened. And it's hard to keep taking from someone like that without giving anything back.

Whatever the problems that kept them apart, Mom adored my father. If she was drinking, her voice might take on a sarcastic edge when his name came up. Every great once in a while, when she forgot I was sitting there in her room, she might get a strange look on her face and mutter the names of some of the actresses in his pictures. But that was about as close as she came to talking him down. And God help anyone else who found fault with him. It would be instant war. If my brothers or I had the poor sense to try to criticize him, she laced into us before the reproach cleared our lips.

"Geeze, it was bad that Dad did—"

"Don't you dare say anything bad about your father! You just keep your mouth shut."

When she was angry, she had a mouth like a truck driver. She could level anyone with it—and she would. I saw her come close to throwing girlfriends out on the street when they were kidding around and took a more or less playful swipe at the old man.

"Well, let's face it, Dixie, he's not the greatest singer in the world."

That was all she had to hear.

"Bullshit he's not! Long as you're in this house, you don't say one word against that man. You do and you're out on your ass."

They shut up on the spot. They knew she meant it.

Mom's loyalty carried over into the way she played out her assigned role as Mrs. Bing Crosby. The part was difficult for her. She was only at ease on her own turf with people she felt close to. I doubt if she ever knew for sure what was expected of her. The role wasn't spelled out in so many words. It simply evolved. Dad wouldn't have said, "Look, I'm a celebrity and this is how you have to act." He didn't play it like a celebrity and never quite believed that he was. He had a certain ironic detachment that kept him from taking it all that seriously. I remember him joking that he expected to hear a knock at the door one day and there would stand the man in the suit, who would tell him, "Okay, Bing, the game is up. We found you out, and you have to give it back." Not that he felt guilty or insecure about his success. He was grateful for it and enjoyed it. It fit him as comfortably as one of his Hawaiian sport shirts.

But from the way Mom handled herself with the press, she seemed to feel that what she had to offer wasn't enough or was not what people wanted. So she had to transform herself into someone else. I watched her try to appear educated and well rounded and outgoing and unfailingly optimistic—all the things she wasn't—and I know that had to hurt. She couldn't abide sham and deceit, especially in the business, and here she was as full of it as every other Tinseltown phony. But she did it. She gave them what they were waiting to hear, and she carried it off without muffing a line.

"Oh, yes, it's wonderful being married to Bing. He's such a wonderful actor and singer and a wonderful guy, a great father and a warm, wonderful human being. I want for nothing, and life is rosy and terrific and wonderful. It couldn't be better."

PERMISSIONS